CHOCOLATE FLOWERS

JORI NUNES

©Copyright 2013 | All Rights Reserved | 3L Publishing | www.3LPublishing.com

Copyright © 2013 by Jori Nunes. All Rights Reserved. No part of this book may be reproduced or transmitted in any form or by any means, electronic or mechanical, including photocopying, recording or by any information storage and retrieval system, without the written permission of the publisher except in the case of brief quotations or except where permitted by law.

Library of Congress Control Number: 2013956168
ISBN-13: 9780991013265
Softcover Edition 2013
Printed in the United States of America

For more information about special discounts for bulk purchases, please contact 3L Publishing at 916.300.8012 or log onto our website at www.3LPublishing.com.

Book design by Erin Pace-Molina.

This book was researched and stories gathered from crime victims. It is a work of fiction. Any names, events or places of similarity is purely coincidental.

To the friends and family who have shown me
unconditional love and support,
especially Joseph, Ryan, Michael, Tyson,
Dariea, Tracy, Sherry, Belinda, Kim, Rocio,
my second mother Camille
and all the innocent victims of crime.

Introduction

A week before Mother died, she told me a story about a conversation she had with her grandmother a week before her grandmother died. Mother looked at me in a way I knew meant that she needed me to really listen and told me the story.

This how the story went:

She said, "My grandmother knew she didn't have long to live from her stage-four breast cancer when she looked at me and asked, 'What would you like from me when I die to show you that there is more to life once you pass?' I felt shocked but responded, 'I would like one of your red flowers to show up the day you die.'"

Mother continued, "A week passed and I went outside to the back patio to water plants and in a pot that had an old tree, a red flower had appeared as red and as perfect as could be, just like the one I had asked my grandmother for. I later found out that my grandmother had passed away around the same time that flower appeared."

Mother then asked me, "Now, what would you like from

me when I die to let you know there is more to life once I am gone?"

I knew my mother had been fighting a rare blood cancer for years, but she often talked about dying so it did not come as a surprise that we were even having this conversation.

I replied, "I want a red flower, too."

Mother smirked and replied, "You do not even like flowers. You are not a 'flower-type girl.' You would like something different — you do like chocolate. I know! Chocolate flowers!" Mother said with a big, proud grin.

I looked at Mother, shocked, and knew there was no way she could arrange chocolate flowers. I just replied, "Sure, that sounds like me all right."

I smiled and looked at her — there she was with such a genuine grin and twinkle in her eyes. I kissed my mother on her forehead and took a long look in to her hazel eyes. I wondered when I would have the next chance to see her and whispered, "I love you."

Mother didn't respond. She didn't look well — she had a tint of green and yellow to her skin and her thinning hair was a dull salt and pepper color, cut extra short and clinging to her scalp. She had no makeup on, which told me she just had no more energy. I began to walk out of her room and turned to look at her. I wanted to run up to her, shake her, and beg her to tell me she loved me and was proud of me. But when I looked at her, she was already sleeping.

A week passed, and I was busy working at my real estate

office. One of my office phones rang, which was a surprise because I normally don't give that number out. I answered it, and it was a man asking for Jori. I told him that I was Jori.

He replied, "I am at your home, and there is no answer. I have a floral delivery for you."

I told him I was 20 minutes from my home and to leave them on the porch.

He said, "I need your signature."

I said, "Just sign my name, and I'll come right home."

He replied, "I can't leave them out; it's a hot day, and they are chocolate flowers. I'll go see if one of your neighbors are home."

I hung up the phone and grabbed my purse when that same phone rang again. I answered it, and it was my stepdad. He sounded upset.

I asked, "Did Mom die?"

"Yes." He sounded shocked.

"I will meet you at your house, Dad."

I grabbed my purse, my cell phone, and yelled to my coworkers, "My mom just died. I am going to go help my dad!"

I got into my silver Honda and drove home. I felt a dumb shock but was anxious to get my chocolate flowers while I wondered how my mother arranged a chocolate floral delivery at the exact time she passed as promised. I arrived home to the note on my door to go to the neighbor on the right. I knocked on the door and a grouchy, older man answered.

Without saying a word, he went to his refrigerator, opened

it, and said, "I think these are for you."

He handed me this large bouquet of fruits all cut like flowers and dipped in chocolate.

"It looks like chocolate flowers," he said with a grin, adding "I had a few, and they are great."

I held my delivery. I opened the small envelope and read the card:

Dear Jori,
I appreciate you showing us homes and although it has been months, I woke up this morning with a thought that we should do something nice for you today. I hope you remember us.
The Johnsons.

This was a previous client who is a pastor. He never knew I had a mother who had cancer nor did I ever mention the conversation about the chocolate flowers. It had been several months since I had heard from this couple who were considering purchasing a home. I called the client, whom I hadn't even spoken to for such a long time. I was confused and wanted to know what made him decide to send me chocolate flowers, and why that day, of all days? He said he woke up and told his wife that they should do something nice for someone. He thought of me. His wife was the one who thought of sending me chocolate flowers.

"Do you believe in God?" I asked Dad when I met with him at home and handed him the chocolate flowers.

He was so hungry from being at the hospital with my mom all day that he hadn't even thought of eating. He sat and ate the entire bouquet by himself without saying a word. At that moment, I knew that the chocolate flowers were for my dad, and at that time I did not know then what I know now: *Chocolate Flowers* "the book" was for me.

The story I am about to tell is a difficult one, but one that deserves to be told. I am — with great courage, honesty, sincerity, and sensitivity — going to tell it to you. I hope that as you read this story you will come to a greater understanding and awareness of abuse and victims of abuse and sexual molestation. It is based on a true story, but I've fictionalized the characters, places and events to protect the innocent. Any similarities to people, places, or events is purely coincidental.

Chapter One

Jason and I had just returned from our honeymoon. We'd had a huge Catholic wedding with over 300 guests at $40 per plate, which, as the caterer said, would "make it a wedding everyone will remember and talk about for years to come." I remember him saying this, all the while nervously playing with the mustache that curled out over each side of his tense smile.

We certainly were not rich, but we wanted the best wedding we could afford, and we wanted this caterer because our first date was at his restaurant, which was known for his cooking and catering the Olympics. Prime rib, sweet potatoes, and spinach artichoke salad with a honey-mustard dressing. Jason and I drank wine as I giggled, and we exchanged glances at each other as our caterer spoke.

We lived within walking distance of the restaurant and held hands as we walked home and discussed the fabulous menu. We should have requested an appetizer for the same price, or at least a chocolate fountain.

"No, he isn't one to negotiate; we're lucky he's even catering our wedding," Jason replied.

We stopped in front of our home — a single-story blue building, with a large yard and huge shade tree. We knew it would be perfect after I had sold a home on the other side of town for a half-million dollars. Although our new rental was much smaller and not on our preferred side of town, it was, at least for the one-year lease we had just signed, ours.

I stopped Jason at the front door, blocked him from coming inside, and said, "Kiss me."

I looked at his tan face and his deep blue eyes, and he did what I told him to do. Our kisses were passionate, and I found myself smiling, opening my eyes, and catching Jason with his eyes closed, his tongue and my tongue moving together as one. Jason had a way of making me feel butterflies just by looking at his face.

"He melts my heart," I always told people who asked how I felt about Jason, who was my first true love.

Although I had previously been married for 12 years, I'd never felt such passion or lust for a man like I did for Jason. Our kisses were always amazing. We would forget anyone else was around. Although we had dated for years, it was always a long passionate, loving and caring kiss that made me smile. Jason would stop to look at my face, place a hand on my cheek, and grin as he kissed me. I never wanted this mad passion to end. He had a way of making my inner soul melt like butter in a way I could not describe, but it felt amazing to be loved by him.

The wedding day was finally here, and I had spent the evening before at the rehearsal dinner. My little brother Jeremy showed up. At the time, he was 28 and still single. He was a nice-looking guy, blonde hair, and a neatly trimmed beard. He was always in excellent shape as he was a personal trainer and took pride in health and fitness.

I looked past my brother to see my biological father arrive. This was a shock to me, because I had barely seen or talked to him growing up. I had rarely spoken to him since CPS had taken me away from my mother. I remembered sitting in the social worker's office, listening to a police officer on the phone with him, trying to convince him to take me to give me a home, as Mother and my stepfather (who I also called Dad) were unable to raise me. I was 14, scared, and unsure what my life was about to become.

Mother and my stepfather never arrived, so we rehearsed as if they were there. My mother had cancer.

I told the bridal assistant, "She'll be here tomorrow."

I lied, not really knowing the answer. It was Jason's idea to have this large Catholic wedding. The reception was just a part of preparing for the big day. I said hello to my father, Dave, as he took my arm to walk me down the aisle. I had forgotten he was so tall and thin. I had secretly hoped he planned to shave the scruffy beard for the wedding. No one else knew how uncomfortable his touch made me, but inside I was glad I wore flat shoes in case I had to run. As we walked, I looked up at his old-man face and thought how he had aged, but the smell of liquor still filled the air between his mouth and my nose. It brought back unpleasant memories that made me wish Jason had not insisted we include him.

When we got home, I called my mother and my stepfather answered.

"Dad, are you and Mother coming to the wedding tomorrow?" I asked.

"I don't know, Jen; you know it depends on how your mother is feeling in the morning," he replied.

I couldn't sleep that night; I was up thinking about how hard it was to purchase my wedding dress without a mother there, and how when I did find the perfect dress another girl who tried on the exact same dress had walked out at the same time. Her mother had cried with joy, and she'd jumped out of her chair to tell her daughter how proud she was of her, and what a beautiful bride she was going to be.

"Your mother has cancer," my friend Sandy reassured me. "She'll come to your wedding, though. You watch, she'll be there."

I smiled, empty thoughts of sadness in my heart for the mother I had yearned for during all those years when I was just a child with a "mentally absent" mother, a mother who had multiple personalities disorder.

The day of our wedding, I took hours to get ready. I pulled up my white stockings and thought, "Is it really fair for a woman getting married at 38 who already has two kids from two different fathers to wear such white stockings?"

Laughing to myself, I also put on my lacey white bra and matching panties. Two of my bridesmaids showed up. Tina, who had been my best friend since I was 15, and Sandy, who I had become friends with while our kids played together. She was also a neighbor from the house I had lived in with my first husband. We were all giggling and talking about the day ahead when I heard a pound at my front door. Tina went to answer it and came back with my mother.

I was shocked to see her, but also upset when the criticism began. "Your legs are way too chubby to be wearing such small stockings, and your fake boobs look pokey in that bra! Are you trying to look like a whore at your own wedding?" she cried in a rather loud voice.

Tina tried to change the subject, but it was too late. I was crying and not just crying, bawling. Sandy tried her best to cheer me back up. Tina walked my mother into the other room while Sandy helped me dry my tears and touch my makeup back up. I even thought that I looked nicer this time.

I looked in the mirror and smiled. "Thank you, Sandy."

My mother was there, and so was the stepfather who had raised me. I wanted them there. I always wished things could just be normal, and that my mother wasn't different from all the other mothers. Everyone I ever loved would share this special day with me and nothing was going to ruin it for me. I took my dress off the hanger and looked at it. It was my goal to wear a size six at my wedding, and there it was — the perfect dress and the perfect size six.

"It is beautiful. Joyce, you need to get in here and see your beautiful daughter!" Sandy yelled.

She tried to get my mother's attention so that she would come back into the room and hopefully have something kind to say. I knew that my mother did not know how to say nice things to me. Just the thought of her coming back into my room to see me naked upset me so much that I pulled the dress up as fast as I could before she could enter my bedroom.

My mother walked in with a disgusted look on her face — as if she had seen a horror movie. The worst, most unimaginable thing happened with one hour until "here comes the bride." I looked down to see bright red blood. I had started my period all over my beautiful, custom-made, form-fitting dress. All over my white panties, all over my white stockings, and all over my fancy white high-heel shoes.

Tina looked as scared as if there was no way to clean all the blood, turned, and looked at Mother, who turned her nose up. She laughed as she walked into the other room to announce it to my stepdad. I heard laughter as Tina grabbed a towel and tried to keep the blood from making a worse mess. Tina and Sandy tried to change the mood in the room as they helped me take everything off and rinse it in cold water. I was even more embarrassed to see Tina and Sandy exchange looks of shock.

"Never fails that she screws up everything in her life!" I overheard Mother announce. "I'll meet you at the wedding and let Jason know you're a bloody mess! Some wedding night you're going to have!"

With that declaration, the door slammed shut. I took Tina's glass of wine and chugged it while I changed back into my now-wet wedding attire.

We barely made it to the wedding. All the guests had arrived. The photographer had a great idea to take a few photos of us (me and the girls) as we rushed around to get ready. I stopped and took a photo with my mother-in-law and Mother. We acted as if everything was fine and nothing had ever happened. Mother seemed different — she was calm and relaxed, and she smiled for the camera with nothing really to say. My dress was still wet, but no one could tell because it was covered in an antique-soft "whispering pink," as the sales woman described it. I heard our violinist begin to play some songs that Jason and I chose, and I found myself all alone waiting after everyone had walked over to the church.

"I have a surprise for you," said the photographer.

My "real" father followed behind her.

"Your dad is going to have a talk with you while I wait for the cue. Then, I'll come back for you."

I began to panic when she shut the door behind her. She thought she was doing me a favor. I looked up at my dad who was at least 6'4" tall, thin, and had a homeless look about him from all of the alcohol abuse over the years.

"It's great you came, Dad" was all I could think to say.

His eyes narrowed down as he stared at my breasts. I nearly blacked out when I felt his hands begin to caress them.

"Your breasts look great. Look at all that cleavage. Your surgeon did a fantastic job!"

"Dad, please don't touch me. I am getting married."

The door opened and our photographer came in and stared at my dad whose hands were still on my breasts. She saw tears running down my cheeks. She ran over to me and handed me a tissue with a shocked look on her face. She said it was time, and we walked together across the parking lot from the bridal room and into the church.

She whispered, "I am sorry" as we walked into the church.

"I will never see him after this day. He will never touch me again," I replied as I wiped the tears from my cheeks.

My stepdad must have seen the look on the photographer's face and then on mine.

He said, "I need a minute to speak to my daughter."

He pulled me by my arm into the coat closet that was in the church-entry area. I told my stepdad, John, what had happened. We agreed I would put a smile on my face — this was the first day of the rest of my life. I was about to marry the love of my life. I would spend the remainder of my life with Jason — and I would think of that and only that. He was right; I needed to get over my feelings and enjoy the ceremony that was about to happen.

The music began with the band playing the traditional wedding song, and the doors opened. I walked down the aisle with both dads, one on each arm. It was the best day of my life, and right that second I knew it would only get better. I walked slowly down the aisle and took the time to look at the guests who came to our wedding. There were relatives I hadn't seen in years, smiling, crying, and looking so happy for me, the bride, about to marry my best friend, my prince charming. About to begin a new and happy future. Today was all about forgetting the past and making the future the best it could possibly be. I didn't care that Jason and I had a small rental home on the wrong side of town. Just as long as we were together, I was happy and nothing could ever change that.

As we made what seemed like a long trip to the front of the alter, my two dads each said something to the priest and then to Jason. I looked at Jason and noticed how hard he had tried to do his hair the way his brothers had always tried to tell him to do it. I thought it was special that he tried so hard to look his best, but my nerves got the best of me. I turned around and looked at the entrance I had just walked through. I wondered how long it would take to run out of there. I was just looking at my long wedding-dress train and thought about how hard it would be to turn it around and run out when I caught the eyes of Jason's grandmother. She looked at me adoringly and blew kisses to me. "Such a sweet and kind little woman," I thought. I smiled at her. I reminded myself, I was not only marrying Jason, but also his family — his big wonderful family with four brothers and eight nieces. There would never be another lonely moment in my life again.

I smiled, blew a kiss back to Grandma, turned, and looked at my mother who also seemed happy. She sat proud with her dark pink dress with the matching corsage that Jason and I had purchased for her, his mother, and Grandma to make them feel special and stand out. I looked into my mother's smiling, proud eyes, and I blew her a kiss. She blew me a kiss back. I turned to the priest and gave him a nod to say, 'I am ready'.

The wedding was a long, Catholic wedding. I stood and felt my still-wet dress and wondered if anyone noticed. The priest had even made a joke about us standing for the entire ceremony not really knowing our reason why. Still, we stood holding hands and staring into each other's eyes, which helped me to relax. Feeling the way his hands felt so rough from being an aircraft mechanic took my mind off what had just happened with my dad. After standing for so long, I heard a crashing noise and then I heard gasps.

Tina, my maid of honor, said, "Cole (my son) locked his knees and fell straight to the ground like a timber tree."

I was not sure if I could get to him fast enough with my wedding-dress train, but before I could move, Matthew — my oldest son — ran over to Cole, sat him down next to Jason's father Bruce, and then went up to take Cole's position at the altar. This was a wedding miracle, because Matthew had protested our wedding and refused to be in it because he didn't want another man in my life as a father figure. He wanted me to stay with his dad Patrick, the man I had married and stayed with for 12 years, the man who raised Matthew as his own and adopted him. The man who "saved us" from our evil past.

After what seemed like forever, our priest announced, "You may now kiss the bride."

Jason kissed me. I kept my eyes open so that I wouldn't miss that moment. The moment that every little girl is told to look forward to. I looked into Jason's eyes as he kissed me and saw him smile. I knew I had just married the love of my life. Everyone in the church stood, clapped, and watched us: "Husband and wife" walking out of the church never feeling more proud. Another new beginning; I was finally Mrs. Devonshire.

Chapter Two

The day I died was the perfect day — it was a sunny day, with no wind. Not too hot, not too cold. The sky was blue-bird blue with white fluffy clouds.

It was a Sunday afternoon. Jason and I had decided to take a ride out into the country before we headed into the city to see my parents. My mother was having a good day, which had become unusual. As if laying in bed with no energy from cancer and having a rare blood disease wasn't enough, she also had weekly trips to the hospital for blood transfusions. This day was different — and this day was good. Mother promised me that she would make her famous fried chicken. I'd always said my mother's fried chicken would be my last meal if I had a choice before I died. It was a meal she'd made when I was growing up on the good days when she would come out of her room and decide to finally be "Mother".

Mother had been in bed and depressed most of her life. She always complained about dying from something. More recently, however it was discovered that Mother had been finally diagnosed with multiple personality disorder (AKA dissociative identity disorder) as well as a rare blood disease called hemochromatosis. Not to my surprise, her therapist discovered several different personalities developed from my mother's disturbing childhood filled with abuse. He never mentioned "the witch" (I think that one is still in hiding from my childhood).

Jason and I had just returned from our honeymoon, a cruise to Alaska. We had zip-lined across the rainforest from treetop to treetop as we gazed down at wild bears that clawed in the streams to catch salmon. We had taken a helicopter ride to the top of a mountain to walk over glaciers. When Jason had leaned over a the edge glacier to take photos, the tour guide grabbed his arm and yelled at him. He had warned him that it was unsafe. We had gone on a boat to whale watch. I was the first to spot four orcas that put on quite a show. Jason even took photos until the camera's battery died. But my favorite event on our honeymoon was when our cruise ship let us wander on an island alone. We walked until we got lost. Holding hands alone while it rained lightly, we got soaked, hugged, and occasionally stopped for a kiss. The rain poured and wet our clothes.

While lost, we discovered a bald eagle rescue museum and watched bald eagles attempt to fly with their injured wings. We walked past a fast-moving river where we just stood, watched the river, and held hands. We kissed in the rain until dark when we missed our cruise-ship departure time and held everybody up from docking. Although we laughed as we boarded late, there was a crowd of passengers who made sure we knew that we held up the trip. They made comments and wagged fingers at us. We just giggled as we ran to our room and held hands like young children in love even though we were in our late-30's.

We had hated that our honeymoon was nearly over, but I had also missed my kids, Matthew and Cole. I really couldn't wait to see them and tell them all about our perfect honeymoon. I had gifts for them that I had collected at each port. Rocks, feathers, marbles, crystals, and lots of photos to show them, but more than that, I wanted to give them hugs and explain how much I missed being with them. This had been the first time I had even spent time without them, and it was 10 fun filled days that just flew by.

But it was over. We were about to experience life as a newly married couple. Everything Jason and I did, we laughed and seemed to always be holding hands. That day was an extra special day — we were going to have our turn to feed the cattle up at the family ranch, a 400-acre lot of land that contained wild horses, lamas, and beef cattle. The animals were hungry from a lack of grass as summer came to an end and fall began.

Although, from the look of that day, you never would have thought of it as fall. The sky was a crystal blue with the whitest clouds I had ever seen. We got to the entrance and I grabbed the keys and hopped out of the truck. I ran to the gate, opened the lock, pulled the large gate open, and watched as Jason pulled the big, ugly white truck with the camper shell past me. I never did like the way that truck looked, I thought. I shut the gate, ran up to the truck, and jumped up on the passenger's seat.

Our dog Trixie was with us. Her tongue hung out as she panted to escape; her stubby tail wagged, and she began to whine. She seemed to know that she was about to be able to run and run. Jason drove up to the feeding area and gave me instructions to drive.

"Follow the truck tracks one mile up and slowly turn back to this spot. Drive slow and keep the window open so you can hear me," he advised.

I let Trixie out and watched her small, white body disappear into the distance. She reminded me of a rabbit as she ran. She got smaller and smaller until I could no longer see her. It was hard to believe she was already 10 — she had the energy of a puppy, I thought as she ran out of sight.

I pulled the truck back and watched Jason load the hay on the trailer from the front seat of the truck. He had a great body and was three years younger than me. I am not sure why, but I was proud of that age difference. Being with Jason made me feel different than anyone I had been with before. He never seriously dated anyone before me and was quite a guy. He never said a bad word about anyone or anything. He was also a virgin when we met, which is very rare in this day and age, but Jason was shy and religious. He wanted to wait for the right woman. He found me, and I was nowhere near a virgin — as a matter of fact, I don't even remember the first time I had sex. You can't call it lovemaking if it is forced. I know my first time had to have been forced because I was too young to remember.

Sex was a part of me. I don't remember life without sex, but I found it refreshing to be with someone who adored me and made me feel a way I had never felt before, almost like I was a princess to him. He was so proud of me that he would introduce me to strangers on the street. I adored him and craved his undivided attention. Love, affection, tender touching, caring, and unconditional love were things I had always wanted and never had before I met Jason.

The cattle were all feeding, and I realized Trixie had disappeared. I looked through the hundreds of acres to find Trixie. She was nowhere to be found. Getting into the big, white, clunky truck, we began heading for the gate and honking the horn until we finally spotted Trixie. She was running around the lake, trying to get the courage to jump in to catch a duck. Trixie's tail was still wagging, and her tongue hung out of her mouth. She looked exhausted and filthy. We laughed when saw how muddy she had gotten. I suggested we let her ride home in the back of the truck under the camper shell. Jason agreed and laughed.

I opened the back camper shell and even popped open the back side window.

Jason asked, "Why are you opening a window? Don't you think Trixie will jump out while we're driving?"

With that, I reached over to shut the window — and it was stuck open.

"Well, if she jumps out, it's not my fault," he said.

"I'll watch her," I replied.

I opened the gate and once the truck was out, I locked the

gate and jumped in the passenger seat. I got on my knees to turn back and see Trixie.

"You stupid dog. Look how dirty you are," I chastised out loud and laughed.

I heard Jason laugh, and then I started to laugh even louder. Trixie was so dirty that her white fur looked brown. It was a great idea not to let her sit up front with us. She was also tired and immediately laid down to sleep.

After a few minutes of laughing, our discussion got serious. Jason and I discussed our wedding gifts and meeting our photographer.

"I'll also have to call my mother to let her know we're running late for fried chicken," I said. "I sure am starving!"

"Honey, is your seatbelt on?" asked Jason.

I rolled my eyes and replied, "Jason, it's 12:00 o'clock on a Sunday afternoon; no one is out here in the country."

I then reached over to put on my seatbelt and just as I did I looked up and saw the face. The strange man stared at us as he drove by, almost too fast to stop. His face appeared right past Jason's face — he looked right at us with his eyes wide open as if he were shocked to see us, too. He drove a white van, which had appeared from nowhere behind a hill. He didn't stop at the sign. Instead, he just stared at us as if he were in a trance.

"Jason, he's going to ..."

For a split second, I thought the driver had missed us — until the truck began to turn backward and spin out of control.

"Is your seatbelt on?" Jason cried.

I couldn't answer. I had never been in an accident — and I was shocked. Things seemed to be going in such slow motion. I turned to see if any cars were coming. I thought, I just didn't want us to hit anyone as the truck now moved backward in the opposite direction.

"I have no control, honey, I'm sorry!" Jason cried out apologetically.

I knew from his voice that he considered this a warning that it was going to get worse before it got better.

I was scared and prayed, "God if we die, please make sure my two sons find my life insurance and that they are taken care of."

I began to think of all the things in life I would be missing out on, my mother's fried chicken, and how we were supposed to be there for lunch in just an hour. My sons' graduations, and their weddings, and my grandchildren. Jason and I had even talked about and planned on having a child of our own.

"We are going to have to get off the road before we kill someone else, sweetheart," Jason said, interrupting my thoughts. "There's another car coming right for us," he explained. "If we stay on the road, we may kill them, too."

I felt the truck lean off the road.

"We're going into a ditch now," said Jason, who sounded calm as he tried to keep me calm and explain what was happening.

I felt it as the truck went right off the road and into the ditch before we went up again and started to spin and flip. I didn't hear from Jason after that so I said, "I love you" as the truck rolled over. I saw the glass on the front window break and the ceiling above us crush inward. This all happened in what seemed like slow motion. Then the truck rolled again to give me a clear view of the sky. The beautiful clear blue sky with the white fluffy clouds, then the grass again, sky, grass, sky, grass, sky — everything I saw as we rolled over and over in the big, white, clunky truck that I hated so much.

I never would have guessed I was going to die on that day of all days, a beautiful sunny day. I said a prayer: "I will miss you Mathew and Cole. Mommy loves you and wants nothing but the happiest lives for you two. I will be watching over you both from the white fluffy clouds above. Please God, come soon and don't let us suffer any pain."

Chapter Three

It was my fourth birthday, and my mom told me, "The day you were born, your dad dropped me off at the hospital and said not to call him unless you were a boy."

I really wasn't sure what she meant by that at the age of four, but it was a tradition to tell me that story every year on my birthday, October 29, 1967.

"You were almost a Halloween baby," my mother would always say.

Birthdays were special. We always got a cake, and my mom was happy and in a good mood on our birthdays. On our birthdays, she was "Mother". Halloween was also great because we never knew what costume Mom would think up to make us wear, but my older sister Tasha and I always looked forward to the surprise. The first year I can remember was when I turned four, my mom made me a duck costume. Yellow feathers, orange stockings with big feet, and a beak to match. My sister was a cheerleader. I remember my mom always took pictures of my sister but for some reason not too many of me.

"You're not the pretty one," she would remind me.

My sister was gorgeous. I didn't know quite what the word meant but that's what my mom always called her, "gorgeous". We would get Mother's special fried chicken on our birthdays, and on my birthday we were given our Halloween costumes, too.

My dad was rarely home; he worked a lot and had to get up early, but he also came home late after having a few drinks with his buddies. We had just purchased a small 1,000-square-foot single-story home on a busy street. It had a family room open to the kitchen, a sofa, and a stand with a black-and-white TV. There was a fireplace with an oak mantel and an old clock on top. There was also a kitchen which we were forbidden to go into, and an area for a table right next to the kitchen, a big den that Dad built from a covered patio area, and two bedrooms with a bathroom in-between that we all shared.

It was a special birthday because dad had come home and made us stay in the backyard to play while he got my birthday surprise ready. My sister and I played on our swing set and took turns going down the slide. She was always so careful of me, like I was her little doll. She would hold my hand while I would climb up the ladder until I sat, and she would count to three and softly push me. She had darker skin than I did, green sparkly eyes, and a huge smile with her two front teeth missing. When she would count, she would spit when she got to three, and we would both laugh and laugh.

Dad called us inside — my present was ready! Holding hands, we ran to our room to find my crib was gone and had been replaced with bunk beds. I was so excited to get the bottom, and my sister was so thrilled to get the top! My mom even smiled even though my sister whispered, "Mom's mad again."

I looked at her, and she smiled and that was good enough for me. The first night was scary because I had a belly ache and was afraid of my new bed, but my dad came in my room and talked to me. He explained it was all right to be scared. He even turned on the bathroom light and left our door opened. He walked out, and I could hear my mom start to yell because the bathroom light was on. My dad came in again, told me he had to turn the light off, and he was sorry. I heard more yelling from my mom and tried to fall asleep, but the screams got louder and louder until I heard a thump and then there was silence. I peed my bed before I fell asleep and slept in my wet pajamas.

The next day my mom wouldn't talk to me. She wouldn't look at me, and I stared at her face.

"Sister, what's wrong with Mommy?"

I was worried when I looked at my mom's face that appeared black and purple, and her eye was swollen shut.

"Don't talk to me and don't talk to Mommy," said my sister as if I had something to do with Mommy's face.

I sat quietly and looked into the bowl of cereal, eating even though I was not hungry. My mom did not talk to me for several days until one night when my dad came home drunk. My mom was giving me a bath, and my dad insisted on watching her bathe me. He pulled my mom's hair back and whispered something into her ear. My mom made me stand up, my dad handed her a washcloth, and made her get it all soapy. He took his pants off, and I saw his penis as he stroked it up and down as my mother slowly washed my body. My mom cried and cried, and I asked her what was wrong but she never talked to me. It felt good having my mom touch me. She never touched me, only my sister — she was the gorgeous one.

Then my mom ignored me and made me sit on my bed every day for weeks as a punishment, but I had my gorgeous sister who would sneak me some of her food. She would come in with her dress pockets stuffed with food, take her hands out, and hand me pieces of bread, meat and squishy peas, carrots, and corn. We pretty much had the same thing every night. Tasha would get a brush from the bathroom which was next to our bedroom and between our parents' bedroom. She would brush my long, tangled hair and always told me that I was her pretty little princess sister. She would reassure me that she would always take care of her baby sister.

We often fell asleep holding each other. My sister was the most important gorgeous person I knew. We would stay asleep until dad came in the room to wake me up. He pulled my arm and my sister cried and pulled the other arm. Eventually, Dad would win, and I would look at my sister and say, "I'll be back Tasha." I didn't want my sister to be scared or worried, and I especially didn't want her to stop taking care of me or touching me.

After what would seem like forever, I would return to my bed, and Tasha would be there, ready to hold and hug me. She whispered things in my ear to make me smile, but I never really heard what she said. I was tired, scared, and my privates hurt. I fell asleep scared that Daddy would come back in and take me again or worse, take Tasha. I would hold Tasha and try hard not to make too much noise because I could hear Daddy snore loud, and I did not dare to wake him up.

Days passed until a day came that my sister ran into our room. She was so excited, "Jenny, Jenny!"

"What, Sister?"

I popped my head up off my dirty pillow, and she announced that Mommy told her she was starting school tomorrow.

"Real school!"

My mom followed behind angry, "You are such a mess! Look at you, you filthy dirty mess."

She grabbed my hair and pulled me into the bathroom and pushed me into the tub that was already filled with cold, dirty brown water. She took a bar of soap and roughly washed me. The water turned browner, but I sat still and looked at my clean legs and started to count the brown bruises and the purple marks from Daddy's hands. Mommy suddenly yelled at me and told me that my legs were ugly, and I was never to wear a dress because my legs were just too ugly.

"You also have an ugly face," she added.

My mom grabbed a towel and began to clean me the same way she did when my daddy was there, but Daddy wasn't there and Mommy dried me all over. Then I felt her fingers up inside of me with the bar of soap as she scrubbed hard and told me I was a very dirty girl — and I should have never been born.

Her fingers hurt, and I felt her ring scratch me inside. I felt blood, and Mommy got madder as she grabbed me from the tub and wrapped a towel around me. She picked me up with the towel and pushed me on the bottom bunk. That was the last time Mother came in my room, I sat on the bottom bunk, wearing that towel for days. I watched Tasha get ready for school, heard Mother brush her hair and talk softly and sweetly to her in the other room. I wondered what it would be like to be Tasha and to be so gorgeous. "She's so lucky," I thought. I lay on my bottom bunk and stared at the top bunk, bedroom walls, carpet, and out the window into the large backyard.

Mother let me go to a department store called Mervyns to shop for clothes for my sister. I was scared of the white fake bodies that wore clothes with no heads and started to scream. That was the first time I remember my mom slapped my face. I remember a lady looked at her but never said anything.

While Mother was occupied and looked at clothes, Tasha leaned over the stroller, smiled, and kissed me. She told me she loved me more than anything, even all her toys. My sister had lots of toys. Sometimes she let me play with them, but they were in the den. Sometimes Tasha would bring me one, but Mother would see it and take it away. She told Tasha that I was bad and couldn't have any toys until I learned to be good.

My sister had a big smile each time she came out of the dressing room. Mommy would smile even bigger and told everyone who could hear about her gorgeous daughter and how great everything she tried on looked on her.

Mommy would pinch me under my arm and yell in my ear, "Stop being a selfish little brat and clap for your sister when she's happy."

So I clapped each time my sister came out wearing a different outfit. My mom brought me into the dressing room and grabbed my sister's clothes. She took a red pen out of her purse and took each tag to cross out the price and change it.

"They are all on sale!" she said with excitement.

My mother would take the clothes to the register and argue with the cashier about the sale prices until my mother got the sale prices she insisted on. Back when I was a child, there were cash registers, and someone would look at a price tag and manually enter the prices. Mervyns would use a red pen to mark down prices, and my mother knew this and would "help them", as she often said. Years later Mervyns went out of business, and I always wondered if Mother had anything to do with that.

Every day, my sister got up early and Mother always helped her. Mother didn't touch my sister the way she touched me. She touched her gently. I watched as she brushed my sister's long, curly blonde hair.

"You have the most beautiful hair," she would say over and over as she brushed Tasha's hair and put it in two pig tails, one on each side of my sister's gorgeous face.

She had a red plaid dress with a white blouse underneath it, white stockings, and shiny black shoes.

My mother got the camera out and began to take photos of

my sister, cooing over and over "You are gorgeous".

My mother left me alone as she walked my sister to school just down the street. I got up, took the brush, and began to pull it through my own tangled hair. I turned around and saw my mother, who stood in the doorway with her hands on her hips and anger in her hazel eyes. She grabbed the brush from my hand and threw it across the room. She ran out of my sight and came back with large silver scissors in one hand. She charged at me and grabbed me by my mousy brown hair and pushed my frail body to the ground. She grabbed my hair and began to cut it all off. I screamed and cried, but Mother just yelled and cut.

There was nothing I could do so I just lay with her on top of me. She was pulling and cutting my hair. I heard Daddy come through the front door. He rushed into my room and looked at me, then grabbed my mother and pulled her into their bedroom by her arm. The scissors dropped to the floor. I could only hear my mother's screams, then thumping sounds and silence. I just sat on my bed in my wet panties. In those days, I got so scared that I wet my pants on a daily basis.

Later Tasha came home and went straight to our room to tell me about her school day. She ignored the fact that my hair was chopped off, and I was half-bald with clumps of hair pulled out from my scalp. She left the room still talking, went into the bathroom, and returned with a cold, wet washcloth. She washed my face and told me all about her first day in kindergarten. She walked out and came back moments later and told me that Daddy said to leave Mommy alone. "She's sick," Daddy later told us.

A few days passed. My sister readied herself for school, and she was left alone to walk down the busy street to the school. She told me it was a big blue school, and there was an old lady neighbor who sat on a chair on her lawn under a large tree. She greeted her on her way to school.

I decided to sneak out of my bed and check on Mother. I slowly opened my bedroom door and walked quietly across the hall to my parent's room. As quiet as I could, I opened my parent's bedroom door and saw Mother laying on top of the bed — her face was swollen and purple-looking. She couldn't open her eyes. She was trying to say something. I came closer and she whispered, "Water."

I went into the kitchen and saw Daddy sitting in the kitchen chair.

"Mother needs water, please," I whispered.

My dad looked up, shocked, told me he would help Mommy, and ordered me back to my room. I heard my parents' bedroom door open. I heard Mommy screaming and crying. I heard slamming. I went to my bedroom door to peek into the family room where all the noise came from. I saw my dad sit on my mother's stomach, and when he turned to see me, he ordered me to come out of my room and come over to him. I stood near Mother, and saw her laugh and cry as he continued to tickle her. He made me take off my clothes and help him tickle Mother. This became a new game for Daddy to play in the mornings after my sister left for school.

Months passed with things being consistent with Dad

always working and Mother staying sick in bed. I just sat in my room while my sister was at school. I waited for her to come home so I could hear about her day. One day, Mother came in to my room and told me I could come out.

"She needs to get used to being outside so when she starts school she'll be able to go off on her own," she told my dad.

I stood there, uncertain if it was a trick, and opened the front door. I wasn't sure what they expected me to do, but I could tell I was supposed to go outside, so I did. I sat on the front porch and looked at the peeling red paint on the house. I could hear my parents argue inside.

I got up and looked around the neighborhood. I noticed the developed large trees and wide streets. I watched cars and began to track the different-colored cars that drove by our small two-bedroom home. We lived on a busy street, and even though we had been living in our house for a while, I never knew our neighbors. I wondered where that nice old lady lived who greeted my sister each day as she walked alone to school. I found a piece of bark and was shocked when a large black dog came right up to me, licking my face.

"His name is Casey," said a strange man.

He wore a white T-shirt under a plaid shirt and blue jeans with buttons in the front. He didn't have a lot of hair and smiled at me.

"What's your name?" he asked.

I didn't know what to say so I just smiled and said, "I like your dog."

He winked at me, grabbed a large box from a truck, and walked into the house next door. I sat on the grass and petted the dog for at least an hour until the man next door called "Casey," and Casey left. When Tasha got home, she was shocked to find me sitting on the front porch. I told her all about the dog next door, Casey, and she sat with me. We talked while we listened to my parents argue. We waited to see if the man or his dog, Casey, might come back out front. We had no idea at that time how the next-door neighbor would change our family's life.

Chapter Four

It was summertime and my sister finished school. She got a few months off for a break. We were home most days. Mom was home, too. She was just in bed, and we didn't see her much as Dad always said she was sick. My sister Tasha and I spent most of our days next door at our new neighbor's house. We liked him so much that we called him Dad, and he didn't seem to mind, but he would laugh and say, "Don't let your dad hear you call me that."

He would just chuckle and work on his bills or a crossword puzzle while we sat around his coffee table to play with his chess set. He said his name was John, but we still called him Dad. Our real dad was never around, and our mom never noticed when we left the house. John often asked about Mom. He would pay us a quarter to tell him everything about her. One day, just after returning home from the grocery store with Mommy, I heard a huge crash from the busy street in front of our house. John came running out of his house with Casey following behind. John looked at my mother bending over into the trunk of her baby blue VW bug. She was picking up groceries.

He yelled, "Hey lady, maybe if you didn't wear such short skirts there wouldn't be so many accidents on this street!"

She turned and looked at John for the first time. My sister and I giggled and ran into the house.

My "real" dad never came home.

"It's been months," I heard my mother tell the welfare worker. "We have no groceries, and we have no money for our bills. He took everything!"

My sister walked around staked chairs, and I sat next to Mom and looked around. I spotted a man who waved a quarter with one hand and motioned to me to approach him with the other hand. I knew my mom needed the money, and she was distracted with the social worker. I walked over to the man.

He was old like a grandpa and had really bad breath as he spoke to me in my face, "Follow me to the bathroom, and I will give you this quarter."

I followed him into the men's room right into a stall. He shut the door behind us, and I watched him pull down his dirty blue jeans. He had gray fuzzy legs that made me laugh. He reached down and pulled off my dress. He left it on the floor and stood me up on top of the toilet. I stood and balanced. I knew what to expect — it was like the attention my dad gave me only it didn't take as long or hurt as bad. After a few minutes, he helped me down and handed me the quarter. He then left me alone nude in the men's bathroom stall.

I pulled my dress on, pulled up my underpants, and walked

out to proudly show Mom the money I had made so we could buy groceries. I had a huge smile on my face and extended the quarter flat in the palm of my hand. I handed it to my mother, who didn't even acknowledge me when she snatched it right from my hand and tossed it in her purse. I looked over at the old man, and he blew me a kiss. He put his finger over his lips to show me not to tell. He was nice to give me the money for my mom so she could be happy.

Mother was pleased to get the food stamps so we went to a store. When we got back, John walked over and began to help my mother unload all the groceries. His face would light up. He was always happy around my mom. He asked her about the neighbors, and they talked and talked. I ran into the house and was helping my sister unpack groceries when I pulled out a box of cookies.

I looked at my sister and asked her, "What is this?"

I had never had a cookie before so she took the box and opened it. She popped a black cookie with cream filling right into my mouth. I couldn't imagine anything that tasted better. I pulled the cookie box open and grabbed another, then another, and snuck the bag closed. I put it in to the cupboard. I hoped Mother wouldn't notice that I had eaten some.

Mother walked into the house with a big smile. I smiled back at her, and she looked at me strangely. She asked me to go into the bathroom with her. She forced me to smile in the bathroom mirror. I had chocolate cookie crumbs stuck in my teeth.

"You stole my cookies, didn't you?"

I didn't know what it meant to steal, but I agreed as usual with my mother. Leaving me standing in the bathroom, she came back with a large, plastic knitting needle.

"Take your clothes off now!" she ordered as she whipped the needle at my head.

I took my clothes off and noticed blood in my panties. My mother had not noticed, but she turned me around and made me look at my butt.

"Look at that big, huge butt! Look at how white it is and your ugly little bruises all over it. Look at the freckles on your chubby, fat little legs! You are a fat, white, ugly girl. You will never have a boyfriend or get married because you are so ugly!"

She took the knitting needle and shoved it into my mouth and then down my throat. I screamed from the scratching feeling that hurt so bad as she forced my chin up and the needle down my throat until I threw up the cookies.

She smiled at me as I hung on the toilet and she said, "Never steal again."

She shut the door behind her. I collapsed onto the cold linoleum floor and cried. I didn't like myself. I hated myself. I was so ugly and such a bad person.

I woke up to a jerk on my arm. Dad was home. He smelled bad like the man from the welfare place who gave me the quarter. He pulled my arm and yanked me to his bedroom. He threw me on top of my mother who was startled when it woke her up. She began to yell at my dad for waking her up. She continued and complained at him for leaving the house for so long and for being drunk. He slapped her on the side of her face, but this time she didn't stop yelling.

"I have a boyfriend! You can't just come back and think I would just let you in!"

As I lay on the bed, I looked at my mother who screamed in my ear as my father once again began to stick his penis inside of me. There was nothing that was going to stop him so I just lay there and waited for him to make his face like he always did right before he was ready to leave me alone. My mom looked at me with disgust and reminded me that I should have been a boy.

"You know, I never wanted you!" she yelled. "Your sister wanted me to have a baby so she would have someone to play with. I wanted a boy."

I reached over, pulled my night gown on, and walked out of my parent's room. I climbed up the bunk-bed stepladder to my sister and woke her up.

"Tasha. Tasha. Tasha, will you hold me tonight?"

Tasha smiled at me and said, "You come lay down with me, little sister. I will take care of you tonight."

I fell asleep. I felt sad but my sister had me safe on the top bunk.

The next day, I heard a knock at our front door. It was a lady from the welfare office doing a home inspection. My dad answered the door. He told her he was home now, and we didn't need welfare anymore. Dad slammed the door and she turned to walk away. When she left, my dad was angry and went straight to my mother's room to start another fight. I had to go to the bathroom. I went in then heard my mom pound at the bathroom door and beg me to open it. I sat on the toilet and felt pain as I peed. I looked at my panties that were down at my knees and noticed they were once again soaked in blood.

Barging into the bathroom, Mother slammed the door shut on my dad and held it closed as he tried to push it open. I wanted to help my mom hold the door shut, but I couldn't move from the toilet. I felt weak, hot, and numb and fell to the floor. Mother gave in to Father. She allowed him into the bathroom. She did not notice my body that shivered on the bathroom floor. I knew this because I woke up and my parents were no longer fighting or even in the bathroom.

I got up and felt weak. I grabbed the toilet to climb up and hung onto it. As I stood up on the toilet and looked out the window, I saw across to our neighbor John's house.

I noticed his window was open so I opened my window and yelled, "John, help my mommy!" I screamed it as loud as I could until I saw his head pop out the window at me. I yelled again, "John, help me!" and the next thing I heard was my dad arguing with John in our house, and then I heard the front door slam shut.

"Joyce, you are safe. Dave has left, and I don't think he'll be back anytime soon," I heard John reassure Mother.

My mother opened the door and hugged John. It was a really nice, long hug. Then John invited us over to eat. My mother was angry when she saw me on the floor and kicked my head lightly with her foot and told me that John expected us to go to his house for dinner. My mother and John had a lot to talk about, and I tried hard to eat but could hardly sit up and told John I felt hot.

John put his hand on my forehead and told Mother I felt very hot. John got another wet rag and set me up on his couch to rest. I heard my mom tell John she was pregnant and was going to have the baby aborted. I told my sister when she came to check on me. We quietly listened about the baby my mother was going to abort. We looked at each other with our mouths open in shock. Mom was going to kill a baby, and there was nothing we could do.

John let my sister and I stay at his house for a few days to take care of me while I was feverish and while our mother took care of stuff at home. It was the best few days of my life. We sat and planned a vacation to Disneyland. John would let me take warm baths with clean water. He never touched or looked at my privates, and I felt safe with Dad-John.

My mom packed up all my real dad's clothes and put them on the front porch. We packed our suitcases and went on our vacation. When we returned home, Dad's clothes were gone. Mom announced to a friend on the phone that she was getting married! My mom's voice was so happy — and she never sounded better.

"We're going to be rich now," she said. "You can have all the chocolate cookies with cream filling you want."

It was the nicest thing my mother had ever said to me. She smiled, patted her stomach, and said, "This one will be a boy, and he will make your new daddy very, very happy."

I felt sad because John was so nice to me. I didn't want a brother to take away the attention John gave me.

Chapter Five

We moved to a small town in the California Central Valley on a quiet tree-lined street. I got my own room. It had yellow-and-white checkered wallpaper and a large window that faced the garden at the back of the house with a creek behind the back fence that was behind the garden.. I felt safe in my own room because my new dad never came in to wake me up. I could sleep the whole night and not have to get up for any reason.

No more screaming came from Mommy's room. As a matter of fact, Mommy was happy then with the baby in her tummy. I didn't see her much because she lay/stayed in her bed to rest and watch TV. My sister and I decided to ask John if we could call him "Dad."

He chuckled, smiled, and said, "Sure."

We giggled and thought of plenty of reasons to call him "Dad". Dad worked a lot so we could have a nice home, food, and clothes as he always reminded us.

"Tomorrow, you start school," he said to me as he handed me a dime and said, "This is to pay for your milk."

Dad was always soft-spoken and had a twinkle in his eye when he spoke. He had also grown a beard. I wanted to be so much like him that I took my ponytails and brought them in front of my chin to look like him.

"Mommy is going to make you lunch, but you have to buy your milk," he continued with a more serious, pay-attention voice and look on his face.

I was excited to start school. No one had ever talked to me about school before. I was excited to go and see what school was all about although a little scared.

The next morning, my sister woke me up.

"You're going to be late for your first day!" she said.

Tasha was already dressed and on her way out the door. I got dressed and grabbed my dime that Dad gave me and went to see Mom. She was asleep in bed.

I walked slowly up to her and whispered, "Mother, I am going to school now."

She didn't wake up so I put my shoes on, put my dime in my pocket, and didn't want to bother Mother about my lunch so I walked out the front door. I walked down the street and sat on the curb — I was lost.

I sat until a woman walked up to me and asked me, "Why are you sitting here and not at school?"

Her name was Mrs. Jones, I had later learned. She walked me to the school office. Then after what seemed like a long time, Mrs. Jones walked me to my class. The teacher opened the door after Mrs. Jones knocked and introduced me. She informed the teacher that I had gotten lost on the way to school, and the office was not sure of my last name because I had no idea I had one. They assumed I was in the second grade because of my height.

Mrs. Jones looked me in the eye and with a smile, wished me a nice day. She had a beautiful smile. I could tell she was somebody's grandma because she had gray hair and wrinkles. She winked at me and waved as she left the classroom. I sat in the far back chair in the classroom. I looked at all the kids — and they were all dressed special. I looked down at my old, worn-out clothes and felt ashamed that I didn't have a pretty dress or braids in my hair.

I couldn't remember my teacher's name, and when she asked me my name I told her, "Little Sister."

"If you don't tell me your name young lady, I will be forced to walk to your house after school and talk to your parents."

"Okay," I replied with an innocent smile.

I was excited that the teacher was interested in talking to me out of all the kids in the class. The kids started pointing and laughing at me. My face turned red. I looked down at my desk, unsure how to respond. The day seemed to last forever. I wanted to go home — home to my room and stay there where the kids wouldn't laugh and point. Home where there was no mean teacher to talk loudly in my face.

I felt nervous and scared. I shook and dropped my pencil, and when I went to pick it up, the lead stuck in my hand. I didn't want to cause more problems or attract more attention to myself, so I didn't say another word the entire day — not even when the teacher asked me to answer a question. I looked down at the carpet and acted like I didn't hear her.

After school my teacher walked me home. It was then I noticed the teacher's actual height. I am sure it didn't help that she wore black, shiny, pointy heels like a witch and her hair was all teased up on top of her head with too much hairspray. I wanted to tell her I liked her hair, but she grabbed my arm and pulled really hard. She was frustrated that I had no idea which house was mine or even my parents' names.

I went around the block three times before I remembered what house was ours. I finally noticed it because of the side-yard gate with my sister's bike. The bike seat had been ripped, but she still rode it anyway. The teacher knocked loudly at the door until my mother finally answered and looked like she had just woken up with her blue bathrobe and pink fuzzy slippers still on.

"What did she do wrong?" my mother asked in an angry tone.

Mother looked tired and wore no makeup, which was getting pretty common. Mother held a baby whom I had not seen up until this moment.

"Your daughter is the devil," the teacher told Mother in a loud voice.

I stood by the teacher with a big smile and felt proud that I had my first day of school and didn't even know what exactly that meant.

I reached out to touch the baby's soft, white blanket with trains and asked, "Is this my brother?"

The teacher looked at Mother and said, "Take care of this devil child. She is nothing but trouble!"

Mother agreed and pushed my hand off the baby blanket. Mother looked angry, closed the door, and softly whispered, "You have done the ultimate crime and will be punished. Now to your room."

I went to my room, sat on my bed, and played with a piece of paper I had pulled out of my pants pocket from school. I don't know what made me put a piece of paper in my pocket instead of the trash, but there it was keeping me company. Ripping it into smaller pieces, I began to play with the shredded paper like the paper pieces were dolls. I must have played for hours when Mother barged into my room.

"You have a visitor! She's here to talk to you about your behavior at school today!"

Mother returned shortly and came back in with the most frightening witch mask on. I knew it was Mother because of her blue bathrobe and fuzzy pink slippers. I was so frightened that my heart felt like it was beating a million miles a minute just over the sight of the witch mask, which was plastic but looked so real with red eyes and a long nose with a mole — and it made Mother look old and scary.

I yelled, "Take it off! Take it off!"

Mother wouldn't take it off, and I screamed until I felt wet drip down my pant leg. I had peed my pants. Mother's voice changed to a voice I didn't recognize.

She said, "You have been a naughty girl. Now take off your wet pants!"

I reached down as I was terrified and took them off and handed them to Mother as my hand shook out of control. Mother took them and found the wet crotch area and smeared the wet pee on my face. There was no use crying. I stood there while Mother, the witch, chuckled and sounded just like a real witch. She wiped my face with my pee. I tried not to cry, but I was still terrified of the scary witch in my bedroom.

I heard the front door open, and it was my sister. My mother pulled off the mask, smiled with a terrifying grin, and skipped into the other room to greet my sister.

I lay back on my bed. I was naked from the waist down and wasn't sure if Mother would be all right if I left my room just to wash my face; but I heard Mother laugh with my sister. My sister sounded excited to share a story with Mother. I snuck across the hall to the bathroom. I looked in the mirror as I waited for the faucet water to get warm. I thought that my mother was right. I was ugly with my paper-white skin and large moles, big blue eyes that were much too large for my face, and my mousy-brown, frizzy hair.

I grabbed a washcloth and couldn't believe all the dirt I had on my face. I wonder when I last took a bath, I thought to myself. I snuck back into my room and began to play with my pieces of paper. I decided to call the paper, "my family."

I played with my family. I listened to my mother talk to

my sister in the sweetest, kindest voice. My sister is so special and so very gorgeous. She is so lucky that Mother loves her so much. I wanted to be just like my sister when I grew up. I thought all about what it would be like to be my sister before I finally fell to sleep.

I woke up to the cold feeling of my blanket being removed. It was slowly being pulled down my body and off onto the floor. It was cold so I reached my hand down to find it, but jumped when I felt the witch's face. I wanted to scream because the room was so dark, and I was alone with the witch! The witch grabbed my mouth with her large hand, holding it shut as she whispered in a witch voice, "Shhhh."

I lay in my bed as the witch pulled my shirt off over my head. My body shook, and I felt confused. Was Daddy back in our new home? Should I scream for Dad John?

The witch then whispered, "You stupid little girl, embarrassing me today."

I was scared and closed my eyes even though it was dark and I couldn't see the witch, I could feel her and I could see her shadow. I didn't like the witch and wanted her to go away. I knew by the witch's smell and her voice that it was Mother trying to scare me. I lay still. I let mother touch between my legs and push her body against mine and rub her legs over my waist. I didn't like the groaning the witch (mother) made but if Mother were anything like Daddy, she would leave soon if I just lay still. Tears fell down my cheeks, and I tried not to think about it.

I lay in bed and looked out my bedroom window. I could see the moon and a few trees behind the garden-area fence. I knew there was a creek back behind that fence, and I wondered if there were any frogs or secret passages to tunnels that would take me far away to a magical place with nice people like Mrs. Jones, who would greet me once I arrived. The witch finally got up and walked quietly out of my room. I don't remember falling asleep that night, but I guess I eventually did.

My mother wouldn't let me go back to school. I got to stay in my room instead. I enjoyed my little pieces of paper that I called my family. I had an escape to dream of another family, and I would be my special, gorgeous sister. Mother would talk sweet to me, give me treats, and play games with me. I would have long hair that mother would brush and tell me I was pretty.

Time seemed to pass the same way day after day as I sat in my room. I looked forward to Mother bringing me something to eat but I never really felt hungry. My legs were long, and my bones showed. My skin was so fair from staying in my room that I could see my veins, and I knew each vein and where they were from and wondered where they were going. My hair started to smell, and I knew that Mother would eventually smell me, too.

I hated when I needed to get clean. I either had to take a bath and let Mother wash me the way my old daddy showed her, or she would take me outside naked with a bar of soap if I smelled too bad for the family's bathroom. Mother would turn on the hose as I stood there. She would then hose me down with cold water. It hurt me to have the hose on so hard right up on my tender skin. Mother made sure I was all wet and left me for a while to wash my body with the bar of soap.

I had to look like a bubble covered with so much soap before mother came back, or I would have to repeat the entire thing all over again. Mother turned the hose back on and rinsed all the soap off my body. I had to sit outside and dry, even if it was cold. Mother didn't seem to care. She said that I was the devil and she didn't want me.

Being outside wasn't always so bad because there was always my sister's dog Cuddles that liked me, licked me, and let me pet him. The dog made my time drying off fun even if I shivered from the cold

I smiled and said, "Hello Cuddles."

The dog never minded sharing his food either. I would let him think I was a dog on my hands and knees and eat right out of the bowl and even drink water, too.

"Thank you, puppy, for sharing," I whispered before Mother remembered to come bring me back inside.

I stayed up at night in case the witch came back. She came all the time, but only on nights that my new daddy worked real late. Whenever Daddy came home early, I knew because the television would be extra loud. I could hear Dad laugh as he took the caps off his beers and read the jokes. I loved when Dad was home because the witch would forget all about me in my room.

Mornings were always the same. Mother brought my sister breakfast in bed, gently woke her up, and told her what a nice day it would be for her. I tried to peek out the bottom crack of my bedroom door to get a glimpse of what my sister wore that day. She always had the prettiest clothes, and my mom brushed her hair and pulled it neatly back into a bun or added a band and even curled the loose hair. My sister's shoes were always shiny and new, and she wore white stockings and a pretty dress. Her favorite color was red, I think, because she wore it all the time.

Mother reminded her over and over how special she was, and I could tell from my sister's voice that she was happy. I knew my sister always smiled when she talked because she was so cheerful. I wanted to see my sister and give her a hug, but I was afraid Mother would send the witch back in my room — and I was too scared. Sister looked pretty and walked past my door, looking down. I almost think she saw my shadow once because I heard her ask Mother about me, but Mother only said, "She's sick." She would then change the subject.

I would go back and play with my paper family until I heard a cry that went on all day. It was normal to hear Mother cry a lot, but this was a constant high-pitched scream that wouldn't stop. I quietly opened my bedroom door, peeked to both sides, and slowly tiptoed down the hall to where the screams came from in Mother's room. I quietly opened her bedroom door. I saw a large avocado-green crib where the screams originated and looked around. No sign of Mother so I approached the crib and saw him — my baby brother. He was crying. His face was all red, and he looked hot and scared. I reached down to pick him up by his arms, but he was too heavy so I pulled, but I had no strength so I just looked down at him and talked to him softly. I didn't know what to say so I told him about my paper family. He liked my story so much that he finally stopped screaming, looked up at me, and smiled.

I heard the front door open so I hid under the crib. I was scared Mother would be angry at me for seeing the baby, and I feared she would send the witch to take care of me. I hid under the bed and listened to Mother's soft voice as she spoke to the baby. I hoped the baby wouldn't tell her I was there, I thought, as I was tucked down as small as I could be so Mother wouldn't see me.

After a few minutes, Mother left and I heard her go to the kitchen. I snuck back out of her room and took one last look at the baby. I snuck quietly but as quick as I could back to my room and sat on the bed. I was smiling when Mother walked in.

"What are you smiling about?"

I got scared, and she said, "I know! So tell me before I have to tell you what I already know."

I was so scared that I confessed to seeing the baby.

The expression on her face changed, and she yelled at me in a voice I had never heard before.

"Are you jealous of your baby brother?" she screamed.

She grabbed me, held me across her lap, and began to sing a lullaby to me. I was shocked and confused. I felt ashamed that I liked the attention. Mother held me softly and took the warm bottle of milk she had warmed for the baby and fed it to me. She sang and gently patted my back. She told me how much she loved me. She told me how much she cared. She told me I was beautiful. I drank the milk — it was good. I didn't remember drinking milk before, but I was hungry and more than hungry. I was starved for attention even though it was the last time Mother would show me love and affection. That day, I got a taste of love — and I liked it and wanted more.

As my brother got older, I began to copy his words and behavior. I tried desperately to get that attention again, but it never happened. One day I lay in my bed screaming and crying like my brother did that day I got the milk, but I don't think mother ever heard me.

Chapter Six

My childhood slowly went by as I tried to listen to television shows and push my ear as hard as I could up under my bedroom door. My bedroom door was always shut. I was afraid to open it, afraid of the witch. When I would hear TV, I heard the *Brady Bunch* and *Little House on the Prairie*. Those were Mother's favorite shows. Mother and my sister watched those shows and sometimes laughed or talked about what was happening so I was able to catch on to what the show was about. But I mostly heard background laughter in the shows.

I still played with my paper family. I also knew exactly how many yellow squares and how many white squares were on the wallpaper that was beginning to peel off my bedroom walls.

I had a "nice room", to quote the exact words my new dad had used when he showed me that I was going to have a room all to myself. I didn't like not sharing with my sister, but I did not have a choice. I had gold shag carpet, a closet, a large window that faced the back of the house, and a view of the garden that Mother spent so much of her time in. My dad even cut down a tree so I would finally get some light in my room.

"She's allergic to the sun," said Mother.

Mother would tell people that excuse when they questioned my existence.

She added, "She's very, very sick with emotional problems. It's safer for her in her room. It's where she feels safest," she said. "She loves to be alone in her room."

I rolled my eyes behind the closed door. It was hard finding things to keep my mind busy as my paper family started to wrinkle without any form. The paper was so thin from playing with the same pieces for years that they looked too tired to use. The paper had almost become transparent, but I couldn't part with my paper family. They loved me, and I loved them. They were all I had to talk to.

Mother had been letting me out. Once in a while, I would see my baby brother, wave to him, and whisper things to him, but I never could remember his name (his name is Jeremy). He laughed at me and watched me clean the house for Mother. Mother spent lots of time writing, putting notes in a bowl, and letting me play. I picked a note that would be neatly folded and have to do whatever was written on it. I normally ended up cleaning the entire house, but I didn't mind because I got to get out of my room — and better than that, I got to see my baby brother.

As time went on, Mother teased me nonstop about my ever-changing body. She loved to get my sister and brother to sing the songs she made up for me as I cleaned the house.

"Moles, moles, craters and holes. BA. BA. BA. BA. Bionic butt, so she can bounce, bounce, bounce, bounce" were the two favorites.

I enjoyed the attention; although negative, it was still attention so I would just smile at my mother as I cleaned. I especially enjoyed cleaning the kitchen. When no one would look, I would lick the plates and drink the leftover milk or juice from a cup. I would even sneak into the garbage can and eat anything that had meat on it. Mother would never allow me to eat meat. She said she didn't want me to grow — she wanted to keep me small so someday a boy might find me attractive and want to actually marry me.

"Imagine that," she would laugh.

"Jelly-bean nipples," my mother yelled to get me up from my bed and started cleaning.

I got up and rushed to the bathroom and ran to her. My bowl would be filled, and the chores were the same just in different picking order.

I began to notice my sister around the house, wearing bikinis.

Mother would brag, "Isn't your sister's body perfect?"

Of course, I would have to agree. Her body was perfect. She was tall, tan, and had long, beautiful blonde hair. Mother had her lie on a beach towel on the front lawn in her various bikinis. Mother watched from the window as men would slowly drive by or a guy on his bike would fall off as he stared at her. Mother got excited and went outside with drinks for my sister and a special spray bottle filled with baby oil to keep my sister's tan as dark as possible. I sat by the window and watched my mother cater to my sister. She invited men over for a closer look.

My mother kept her camera ready with film. Back in those days, there was no digital; you bought a roll of film, put it into your camera, and took photos. Once the film roll was used, you had to take it to a store and have the store develop and print each photo. You didn't get to choose which ones you wanted or didn't want. You took 24 photos, and you got whatever developed. Mother had a special album for my sister's photos. Mother didn't take many photos of the baby so sometimes when she wouldn't look, I snapped a photo of him.

Mother always said, "How did that one get in here?"

I turned my back to her as if I hadn't heard and smiled to myself. I loved my baby brother, and I wanted to hug him, but I couldn't risk another visit from the witch.

One day, a man knocked at the door and introduced himself to my mother as Keith Smith. He claimed to be a top modeling photographer interested in taking professional modeling photos of the "model" in the bikini on our front lawn.

"She will have to take a trip with me during the summer to Hawaii where we will photograph other top models," he explained. "It'll only be a week."

Mother agreed with excitement as Keith handed her his business card. Mother also insisted he stay for dinner so he could properly meet Tasha.

Mother walked Keith to the door with a great big smile and said, "See you tonight, son" in a flirty way.

She shut the door. Keith then spent the next few minutes to staring adoringly at my sister and admiring her in her bikini as she lay on the towel. Then he got in his fancy red sports car and raced off. Mother happily opened the front door and called my sister into the house to inform her that she was to shower and get ready for her date with Keith.

"You mean that old, fat man who was staring at me just now?"

"Now, now, Tasha. You need to think of it more like the rich, successful man who's going to take you to Hawaii and turn you into a super model!"

Tasha and mother went back and forth as they argued over the age difference of 20-plus years and Tasha's tender age of 13. Mother insisted Tasha be on her best behavior or else. She warned her as she helped my sister pick out just the right clothes and get ready. I lay on my bed and wished and dreamed someone, anyone would discover me.

"Tasha is a popular student, cheerleader, and up-and-coming model," Mother proudly bragged to Keith as we all sat around the kitchen table.

It was a special occasion, and Mother let me sit with the family with the strict orders that I stay silent. I was even allowed to take a bath in the main bathroom. Tasha found a dress that seemed too small and let me dress up. Tasha and I talked about how Tasha really didn't want to go to Hawaii with this stranger, and how she was scared that mother would want her to marry him.

"I can't stand that old, fat man," she said and laughed as she tied my hair back.

We then made up a whole plan. I would look as good as I could so I could get discovered, too. Then I could go to Hawaii with my sister and also become a top model. I couldn't help but dream of leaving the house as I looked at Keith and tried to get his attention, but alas he seemed only mesmerized by my sister.

My sister sat quietly in her pink strapless dress that exposed her tanned shoulders. Her hair was pulled back, and Mother placed a real pink rose to a hairclip on the side of her hair and added the same-colored lipstick.

"Perfect!" Keith continued to agree with Mother's positive remarks about Tasha.

"Maybe you wouldn't mind if Tasha and I went to the mountains this weekend to get to know each other? I could take sample photos of her, and you can see the type of work I do. We will have to have a portfolio ready for her with the best photos. She will need to dress casual and pose in plenty of swimsuit shots. I would also recommend lingerie photos as much as I hate to tell you, all the real super models have those types of photos in their portfolios."

Mother just smiled and agreed, "Looks like we're going shopping tomorrow, Tasha."

My sister looked at me as if I could somehow save her.

"I love shopping. I love photography, and I love to travel,"

I said with my head down, afraid of the rejection.

Keith acted as if he hadn't heard a word I just said, and Mother gave me a kick under the table and smirked.

"My husband is never home. He works all the time at his business. He's a businessman, you know," said Mother.

I could tell Mother wanted to say anything just to change the topic. Tasha looked at me with disappointment on her face, but she knew I had tried to get Keith's attention. After dinner, Keith asked my mother to walk him out to his car. As they left the house, Tasha fell to the floor and cried. Jeremy, Tasha and I hugged each other. We were all crying. We were siblings who didn't have the chance to see or talk to each other. Mother managed to isolate us. I believe this was our moment to let each other know we loved each other before Mother came back into the house. We heard Mother walk back up to the front steps and then the sound of the doorknob move. We all scattered back to our respective bedrooms.

I lay in my bed and dreamed of my sister's exciting modeling career. I thought of how proud mother would be to show her magazine photos to all her friends and neighbors. I looked out my window at the large, white house across the creek from ours. It was nearly eight o'clock. I knew their lights would all go off as if they were on timers. Sure enough, they went off. My light would stay on as I played in my room and kept myself entertained. I would do anything from count the squares on my wallpaper to play with my paper family that were now of little use as there wasn't much left to the paper. I began to imagine that someone in that house across the creek paid attention to me. They turned off their lights so they could spy on me in my room. I began to convince myself that I was someone's entertainment.

Summer was here and that only meant my sister was going to leave on a trip of a lifetime with Keith. Keith was no longer a stranger to our family since he had come around several times a week, picked up my sister for outings, and occasionally took her friends with them. Mother had called the local newspaper and had them print a story about Tasha being "discovered," and although Tasha was used to the attention and Keith, she still was not excited about her summer vacation.

She had been walking around with her head down. Mother followed her around. She tried everything to get her to smile. Mother would not accept the fact that this was not Tasha's "dream vacation," as mother called it.

Keith had come to the door for Tasha, and mother hugged and kissed him. She thanked him over and over for taking Tasha. She reminded Tasha to be on her very best behavior. Mother handed Keith a bottle of the homemade spray tanning oil and began to instruct Keith on how to apply it as Keith acted anxious to get Tasha going with him.

I tried to get Tasha's attention before she left, but I couldn't make eye contact between Mother and Keith at the front door blocking her. I never got to say goodbye to my sister. That summer was going to be a long one. Mother wouldn't know what to do without Tasha, and Mother was about to go through the worst depression she had ever known.

Chapter Seven

A week had passed. I could feel Mother's sadness that Tasha was gone, and Keith had not called as promised. One week soon turned to weeks, and Mother's depression worsened. I kept my bedroom window open to smell the roses and to watch Mother trim the roses back and cut as many as she could for the vases in the house.

I loved to watch Mother sit and garden. She was in her own little world. She usually wore shorts and a tank top, no bra, and a large oversized hat. Mother would get a nice tan although she freckled; too, her shoulders were covered in them.

The rose garden was right outside my bedroom window. It was as large as my bedroom. Beyond the rose garden was a fence that separated the garden from a large creek with the back of homes that faced ours but at a distance.

Mother turned to look at me, smiled, and said, "Come on out here with me, Jenny," in the sweetest voice, as if she were talking to my sister. "I want you to see something. Bring a plastic bag."

I went to the kitchen, grabbed a black garbage bag from under the sink then went out back to see Mother.

"Listen, do you hear that?" Mother asked softly.

I listened and heard soft cries.

"Now, come with me. There's a litter of kittens, and I want to you to help me with them," she said.

I followed Mother to the back gate that led to the creek. She opened the latch and then pushed the gate open. I had never actually seen the creek except from my bedroom window where I tried to see it through the fence posts. I followed her down a dirt path near the creek to an old tree log where the kittens mewed.

"Where's the mother?" I asked.

"I took care of her already. I was waiting for you to help me. Now pick up the kittens and put them in the bag; let's bring them to the main bathroom. I'll get the water ready. We'll give them a nice bath."

I did as mother asked, and when I arrived in the main bathroom Mother's face had changed from sweet and concerned to angry and mad as she ordered me to hand her the bag. It scared me, but I did as I was told. I was afraid to anger Mother. Mother took the kittens and dumped them from the black trash bag and into the cold bath water. As they cried for air, Mother held them down and screamed at me to help her, which I did. We held the kittens down under the water until they stopped crying and the last one stopped wiggling.

I cried for the kittens as I helped Mother.

Mother's face changed again as she began to yell at me, "Go to the kitchen and grab a knife!"

"But they're already dead," I replied in a panic.

Mother slapped my face for the second time in my life. I knew it would get worse if I didn't listen to her. I got up and ran to the kitchen, grabbed a knife from the knife block on the kitchen counter, and ran back to Mother. Mother grabbed the knife and began cutting around the kitten's heads. Mother showed me how to skin their furs. She was laughing as she tore the skin off the kitten's bodies. She told me she was going to fry them and make me eat them.

She looked evil and serious, and I was not about to argue. I was covered in blood and kitten parts. I was past the point of crying or trying to bargain with Mother. Mother had me clean the bathtub and put the kitten parts back into the black plastic trash bag. I walked outside to the garbage can to empty the black bag, still upset and confused. I opened the garbage can lid and saw the mother cat — she looked half-dead up at me and cried in pain but with hardly any voice. She was a brown tabby with green eyes. I was afraid to tell mother so I put the bag on top of the cat and closed the lid.

I sobbed, "I am sorry cat. I am sorry kittens. Please forgive me."

We had kittens for dinner that night. Mother acted like it was fried chicken. My little brother ate two pieces, and I could not eat. I never felt so sick or disturbed in my life. Mother had taken the remainder of the kitten meat off the bones and mixed it in some rice on a plate for Dad's dinner when he came home.

He was exhausted from working all day and could hardly make it to the table, but Mother smiled and said in the sweetest voice, "Honey, dinner is served."

She helped him eat and assisted him to the bedroom after he had relaxed with a few beers. I was able to stay up with my little brother, and we played with some of his toys.

Mother came into my brother Jeremy's room and threw a pair of pajamas at his face, looked at me, and sharply spoke, "I am exhausted. You take care of your brother."

I was more than happy to do so. We stayed up late. Although I did not know how to read, I turned the pages on his books and made up stories to get him to laugh and be happy. I held him until he fell asleep, and I couldn't stop rubbing my cheek on his.

As I rubbed his cheek, I whispered, "Snuggle, snuggle, snuggle."

He fell asleep but would smile at the touch of our cheeks.

The next morning Mother was in a much better mood. She took a bath with the door wide open.

"Jenny!" I heard her yell to me, and I opened my bedroom door and went into the bathroom.

"Jenny, sit down; I want to talk to you," she said in a kind, loving voice.

She began to talk about her abusive childhood. How she didn't know how to be a perfect mother. She went on and on.

I never really listened when she did this because she would never stop telling me over and over about her abusive upbringing and how upsetting it was to her. How she was going to die, and how I should help more around the house. It all sounded like "blah, blah, blah" in my head.

Normally, my sister would sit on the toilet and listen to mother rant on and on while I heard all the stories from my bedroom across the hall. This time, I sat on the toilet, watched her get a washcloth, and get it wet and soapy. I watched her wash her entire face and body. As she finished her story about whatever she was talking about, she would have me wash her back, then wring the washcloth out and lay it over the tub to dry. Mother ran some more hot water, took her hand, and began to rub her own breasts. She told me how good it felt — and that she thought about my sister in her bikini laying on the lawn for all the men to lust after.

"Your sister is so pretty, you should be so proud," she cooed.

Mother moved one hand down to her hairy area and put a finger deep in between the middle where my old dad used to put his penis. She moved it faster and faster, and lay back with her eyes rolled back into her head until she made a face like she had just sucked on a lemon. Then she smiled and opened her eyes. It was amazing. I never saw mother so happy with such a satisfied grin that I, too, wanted to have that feeling.

I wanted to be happy and feel good, too. So I started practicing in my bedroom at night after the lights went out in the white house across the creek lights. It was my time, and I imagined it was my show, and the family would turn out the lights just to see me give a show and display my happiness. I became really good at it night after night and sometimes even invited Mother to watch.

Mother told me things to do to improve. She would sometimes bring me sexy panties to wear and get in the mood. My lights were always on throughout the night. I lay on my bed and played with my 12-year-old body and rubbed my hands up and down my newly developed breasts. I imagined I, too, was a super model, posing for magazines on top of my bed. I tried to make the same faces that Mother did — and I would try to smile the way Mother did.

Mother took an active interest in my newfound sexual ability. She even took pictures and walked me through the movements until I got good enough for a boyfriend.

"You are not going to get a man with your brains because you don't have any, and you're not going to get a man with your looks because you don't have any. If you want a man, you're going to have to get him with your sexuality because that is all you have — and that is all your man will ever want from you."

After Mother left I laid in bed and noticed a light on in the upstairs bedroom from the house across the creek. It flashed on and off to get my attention. I waved and then the lights went out for the night.

As weeks passed and still no word from my sister, my life began to change. Strange packages began to arrive at my bedroom window. They were wrapped in the nicest paper with bows but never a card. Mostly it was lingerie, panties, bras, shiny high heels, and lots of other toys and treats. I enjoyed chocolates and cookies and would often sneak some to my brother. I enjoyed the presents and used everything for my sexual education. I hid the gifts under my bed so Mother would not know about all the extra treats I received.

I waited for the lights on the white house to go off and start my show. I slowly took off whatever it was I wore and put on my lingerie, stockings and high heels. I touched my body all over as I dressed. I bent over and rubbed myself the way the girls did in the adult movies Mother made me watch with her so I learned what to do to get a man. I played with my hair and opened my mouth in a suggestive way, smiled, and played on my bed with different sexual toys. I made sure my "fans" across the creek got a view of the show.

I knew I pleased them by the lights that blinked on and off. When the third light blinked off and on, I knew my show was over. This was a nightly show for months, something I had to look forward to. The only thing I had to look forward to until a gift arrived with a new twist, binoculars.

Chapter Eight

Two weeks had passed and Mother had finally gone to the police to file a missing person's report. She told the police all about Keith, how he took Tasha to Hawaii to model for a week, and it had been weeks with no calls. The police looked at each other and asked mother for any recent photos of Tasha.

"Your daughter's description fits the Jane Doe we have been trying to identify for the past few days."

Mother looked at the police and then at the photo. It wasn't her, thank God.

"He better have a great excuse when they get back," Mother yelled at the police as we walked out the door.

Mother noticed a bulletin board with a letter attached, which asked for a volunteer babysitter. A single mother with four kids needed a sitter during the day. Mother took the letter, and when we got home she called.

Mother started babysitting kids early in the morning. She even let me go with them to school. I liked school even though I sat in a chair and never really paid attention. I looked around at all the students, and my mind wondered off as I thought of different things. The classroom I was in was called "special education" and most of the kids had disabilities, but I didn't mind because I also got to sit in on regular classes, too.

I liked getting out of the house and out of that bedroom. I liked my nice teacher and began to like the books she read. I also got to go to the cafeteria at lunch and sit on the stage step to sell milk for .10 cents. I felt proud taking the dimes from the other kids and handing them milks. This was something I looked forward to every school day.

Mother was really good to the kids she babysat. I liked them — they took attention from her, and she forgot about me. I still sat in my room and listened to Mother read and play with the kids. I heard laughter as I just sat in my room and listened to the things the kids got to do like run through the sprinklers or play dress up. I wondered why I wasn't included.

I was lucky to be back in school and appreciated each morning. One day as I got ready for school, I heard Mother in the bathroom with one of the kids. He cried, and she talked like the witch. I could hear him beg her to take off the mask and to stop touching his penis.

He cried, "The water is so cold."

That was the last time Mother ever babysat that boy. I wasn't sure which one it was, but I felt guilty it was him and not me. At least I knew what to expect and how to get Mother to finish her game faster. I cried that day on my way to school. The teacher couldn't get me to talk. She said some days are just sad.

My sexual evenings began earlier as the lights blinked on and off in the house across the creek. When my clothes were off, I started my masturbation show. I learned to use vibrators and rub lotion on my legs real slow. Mother soon joined the show. She sat on my bed and enjoyed being my audience. Mother apparently came to understand the neighbor's enjoyment in it. She seemed to approve.

She asked me things like, "How does it feel?"

Mother used the binoculars and made hand gestures to the neighbor across the creek. We didn't know him, but he became our friend. Mother said there was just a man who stood in the window, and he was actually cute.

"I bet he would like your sister," she said as she remembered Tasha was gone.

She looked sad.

Dad was on a business trip. He had promised he would get me something special. I looked forward to his return. He kept Mother busy at night so I could sleep and not miss so much school from late-night "shows" with the neighbor.

Mother had a great idea to invite over the neighbor across the creek. She said she was going to meet with him and see if he wanted to join our parties. So that next night, I met Jim. Mother brought him right into my room. I was shocked because he was an older man with blonde hair, a clean-shaven face, a decent body with muscles, and a nice tan.

He said he had a wife and kids but preferred to not touch his own kids because they would put up a fight. He enjoyed my youth, and how I knew how to please myself. Mother pulled off his shirt and rubbed his chest. I laid on top of the bed and looked up at my bedroom ceiling as Jim pulled off my jeans and put his penis inside of my vagina. It really hurt because I felt dry so Mother took some Vaseline and rubbed it on Jim's penis as he took it out of me.

I watched as Mother kissed Jim on the lips and put his hand on her breast. I think she got angry when he took it off so quickly and turned to look and touch me. Jim gave me special attention like I had never had before. I wanted to be his girlfriend. Mother began to call me a dirty whore, which seemed to get Jim to push himself deeper and faster inside of me until he was finally done. I was glad it was so quick, but Mother looked angry.

Jim crawled out my bedroom window, hopped the fence, crossed over the creek, and went into his house. That was just the beginning of my "love affair" (well, that's what I thought it was at that time) with Jim, the married man with a wife and kids; but he gave me all of his attention every night in my room. Mother began to ignore me more, but Jim brought me treats and clothes, and said he loved me and would even marry me someday. I looked forward to this dream becoming a reality. Someone actually does want me.

One day, Mother opened my bedroom door with excitement, "Your sister has been found and is on her way home!"

The police brought her home later that day. I hardly recognized her. It had been months, and she looked thinner than me. Her hair was dyed brown, and she even acted like a different person. She was found in a hotel room, chained to a bedpost. By the looks of her arm, she must have spent the entire time in that condition. Keith Smith was arrested but made bail.

"We will contact you once we have a confirmed court date," officials told Mother.

Mother was more upset with the fact that Keith had not gotten Tasha a modeling job or even paid her for her time. Tasha tried to tell Mother about the things Keith had done to her, the knife, gun, and rape, but Mother wouldn't listen. Finally I held and comforted Tasha.

"You are so fat, Sister," Tasha said with a giggle. "You look like Mother when she married Dad." We looked at each other and both at the same time realized — I was going to have a baby. My sister and I sat on my bed, and I listened to her story about Keith who tricked Mother to let her go with him. They never did anything but go to the hotel where he tied her to the bed and where she had her first sexual experience — and how awful it was.

I told her all about my boyfriend Jim and all the dates we had had with Mother, and how he loved me and would do anything for me. I told her this with a proud smile. I was so in love.

"Now he's going to have to leave his wife and marry me. We're going to have a baby," I thought.

Tasha and I stayed up all night and caught up. Dad returned from his business trip the next day and was more upset about Keith than Mother. He said he was going to make sure Keith paid for the crime.

A few days had passed since I had seen Jim. Finally, he showed up with my mother. He said he wanted to play something different. Mother made a special drink for me, and she made me finish it all until I felt dizzy and fell back on the bed. Jim held my arms down while Mother poked a sharp hanger up my vagina. This was the worst pain I ever felt. I screamed bloody murder it hurt so badly. Jim kept kissing me, telling me, and reminding me it would be over soon.

After what felt like forever, Mother looked at Jim and said it was over. I was told to rest and drink a beer Jim had brought. I slept for days on a pile of bloody towels. Mother continued to care for me, changing the towels. She said I had lost the baby and wasn't sure if it was a boy or girl because she couldn't tell.

Mother didn't like taking care of me. She got frustrated and began to call me a whore as my infection worsened. She said she wasn't about to waste insurance money on me for being a whore. She brought me to the bathroom, washed my body with Pine-Sol®, and scrubbed me as hard as she could with a bar of soap. She shoved the bar up my vagina and told me to lay on my bed with my legs elevated to let the bar evaporate and clean out my infection.

I did what I was told, but the bar evaporated and the infection worsened. I began to smell. One of the mothers of the kids walked past my bedroom door and must have heard my cries because she walked right in and helped me to get dressed. She walked me right out the front door — Mother never even noticed. She took me to the hospital where I stayed for days to recover.

Mother showed up with a story about my infection. She said I had gotten pregnant from my boyfriend and lost the baby at home. They let her take me home with a prescription of antibiotics. That night, Jim came in through my window with flowers and told me he was moving out of state with his family. I would never see him again. I cried and cried and begged him not to go. How could he leave me? We were so in love! He said that everything in life happens for a reason. He promised he would come back for me if he couldn't work things out with his wife, but he couldn't leave her because of their kids.

Loneliness was the worst. Mother was busily helping Tasha get back into modeling. She worked hard on Tasha's self-esteem. It was like Mother just forgot about me in my room. The kids still came over. Mother hardly charged their parents for watching them. She would sometimes do nice things with them like pack them all up in her car and go to the park or the beach.

I was sometimes invited to go, but my depression worsened after I didn't hear from Jim. I just wanted to stay in my room and think about him. Mother found a lost parakeet, and that bird kept me busy for the remainder of the summer. I named him Timmy and taught him to land on my shoulder and say a few words. Timmy was my new love, and I adored watching him learn new things and fly around my room.

He sometimes started a conversation with a stuffed animal.

He especially liked the mouse with the black plastic nose that Jim once gave me. He sat on the nose and just had the longest conversations. I never cleaned Timmy's cage so a mouse made a nest in the bottom of the cage and had babies. I was so excited until Mother noticed them and took the entire cage, Timmy and all. Lucky for me, she returned my bird with a clean cage.

Mother changed and became so nice. She sat on my bed and told me I was pretty. She was going to let me take a bath by myself and let Tasha do my hair and makeup. Mother told me she loved me and was going to take modeling pictures of me that night after a special dinner. We were also going to have company. Mother said someone from the hospital where I had my infection was coming to check on me and do an evaluation for Child Protective Services (CPS).

I was excited with all the new attention that I wasn't thinking about my evaluation, just all the fun we were going to have. Tasha let me wear one of her dresses and did my hair and makeup as Mother cleaned my room and changed my bed sheets. Tasha and I got to play with our baby brother Jeremy. We put him in his wagon and ran around the house and laughed.

The CPS lady was nice. She had a pretty blue dress, nice black heels, and extra-long eyelashes. I was having so much fun and didn't want to talk to the company at all. After observing and writing notes, she didn't stay long. She enjoyed Mother's famous sugar cookies, but before she left she said to my mother that my real father Dave was going to take his daughters on a court-ordered visitation this Saturday.

My sister was excited, but I was scared he would hurt me or Mother again.

"I guess if Tasha is with her, she'll be fine," Mother told the worker as she walked her to the door.

Mother pointed her finger at me and then to my bedroom door. She said she had a headache and couldn't handle the noise. So, I went to my clean room and played with my bird, enjoyed my clean sheets, and waited for Saturday for Dad's visit. I wondered what he looked like and hoped he didn't still smell of booze or try to touch me.

Chapter Nine

Mother stayed in her room when Dad Dave knocked at the door. Tasha and I were ready for hours as we waited. He was very late. He said there was traffic going over the Bay Bridge, and he almost had to cancel, but he had already paid the toll and rented the car.

He gave us each a box of cough drops. He told us that we could eat them all because they tasted like cherry candy. So we both got into Dad Dave's rental car, sat together in the backseat, and ate our candy. We didn't know where we were going, but we were excited to go somewhere.

It was a long drive. I sat in the seat behind Dad. He kept taking his hand, rubbing my knee, and asking us how we were and what we have been doing. We ended up at a creek where dad rented a boat and took us down a long river. He even let us jump out and swim in the river. I didn't know how to swim so I hung onto the boat but could feel the bottom of the riverbed with all the mud and rocks so I knew it wasn't too deep.

Dad never said much other than he was trying to stop

drinking and that he lived in the city (San Francisco), still worked at the same job, and had panhandled. He finally decided it was time to get to know his girls.

My sister and I looked at each other and started to giggle. We pulled our boat over and found a picnic table at a grassy park shaded by huge pine trees. He opened the cooler he had brought and offered us each a soda and a sandwich that tasted good. Soft, white bread with mayonnaise, a piece of ham, and some cheese. Dad even brought plastic bags and handed us each one to clean up other people's garbage. We thought that was a great idea.

My sister got up to stretch out, and Dad said, "Tasha, your posture is not right for being a model. You need to hold in your stomach and stand straight like your sister."

I nearly fell over to hear my dad talk about me as if I were better than my sister in any way. My sister looked upset at him so I told her that I thought her posture looked perfect, and she smiled. I could tell she tried to hold her stomach in and walk straighter and taller that day. I felt bad for Tasha but also couldn't help but feel proud that I was doing something right. I think I enjoyed that day with my dad. Tasha and I talked the entire drive home. We even made plans to spend more time together and explore the creek behind our house.

The new school year began, and I found one friend, Marie. She was popular with the kids. I felt proud that her mother bought us matching cowboy hats and football jerseys to wear to school. Marie even surprised me with a Minnie Mouse book bag. I felt pleased as I walked from my house to hers every morning so we could walk together to school.

But I made a dreadful mistake and told Marie about something I should have kept to myself — my sexual relationship with Jim. One day, I knocked at her door and her mother answered. She told me I could no longer be friends with Marie because Marie was a virgin. Marie had told her mother about my relationship with Jim.

I walked to school alone and cried. My only friend couldn't even be my friend because of Jim. I started to hate Jim and hate my own mother. I got to school and couldn't remember where my class was or even the name of my teacher. I went to the office and couldn't find the words to ask what to do. I felt weak and fell to the ground. I later was informed it was a heatstroke. I felt embarrassed that people looked at me and talked about my passing out in the office.

Rumors started that I was taking drugs and drinking alcohol. I tried to stay at my last class as long as I could to avoid being seen walking home alone. I heard noise from the gym and that's when I met Ron. Ron was one of the most popular boys in school. He was on the football team, and I noticed him look at me and talk about me.

I said, "Hey Ron," and we talked for a while.

He told me he thought I was a cool chick and wanted to hang out at my house so I agreed. Ron walked me home that day. I was worried about what Mother would say or do so when we got to the door, I walked in and asked him to wait. I went down the hall to Mother's room and asked her if it was all right if a friend I met at school came to visit. She agreed and said to stay in the family room so I went back to the front door and let Ron in.

He smiled and tried to kiss me the second I let him in after he noticed no one was around. Just then, I noticed the shocked look on his face. I turned around and saw Mother who was wearing a see-through nightgown and skipping up the hallway from her bedroom toward us. She sang a song titled "Pocket Full of Picks Rice" or something like that. I was so embarrassed I wanted to die. She kissed his cheek and introduced herself as my younger sister "Samantha". Ron started to laugh and thought it was a joke, but Samantha touched and danced around him with a playful look on her face.

I quickly asked Ron to leave.

Samantha started to cry to Ron. She asked him to stay.

She even told him she would stay out of our way, but he looked at me with his eyebrows raised, shook his head, and left. I went to my room and slammed the door, but Samantha followed me and brought some of Tasha's dolls with her. I played dolls with Samantha. It was fun until Samantha decided to be Mother again and ordered me to clean up the mess and return Tasha's dolls back to her.

"What are you doing with your sister's toys? You are always so jealous of her!"

Apparently Mother was back, and so I put Tasha's dolls in her room. I felt confused but that was my life — full of confusion.

I continued to walk to school and sometimes passed Marie

who ignored me. I went to school whenever I woke up and felt like it. No one told me I had to go, but staying home was confusing and boring. I would wake up, get ready, and walk a few miles to high school. Sometimes I forgot what class was starting so I would just walk around the halls or creep into a class with other students and find an empty seat. I didn't know how to tell time or how to read so I would just sit, and sometimes I even learned something.

Mother had decided to make her famous fried chicken and wanted us all to sit at the kitchen table. Dad had announced that he was taking Mother on a trip for the weekend and that Tasha and I were old enough to be home alone. They would bring our brother with them. I was excited for the chance to do whatever I wanted and stayed up that night. I decided to catch up on television shows.

On the way to school, Ron walked past me.

"Hey, Ron," I yelled and he ignored me. "Ron, my parents are going out of town, do you want to come over and hang out with me tonight?"

Ron turned around and said, "Your crazy mom isn't going to be there, right? So ... only if we can have sex?"

I responded, "Sure!"

He smiled and left for class. There was nothing I wanted more than to have a boyfriend. Someone who would love me like Jim did. When I got home that day, Mother, Dad, and my baby brother Jeremy were already gone so I took two hours to get ready.

I told Tasha that I had a date with the best-looking guy on the football team. She looked at me, shocked, and said she was going to her room to sleep because she felt sick. I heard a knock at the door. It was Ron and another eight guys from the football team. Most were black guys that I had never even met and another guy was a tall white guy I remembered from a class. They all barged in and made themselves at home. They cooked eggs on the stove, drank all the milk, changed the channel on the television, and rummaged through my parent's room. One of the guys found Dad's gun and decided to hold it up to my head.

He said, "I am not leaving until I get what I came for."

So I took my pants off and lay on the floor in the family room. I hoped they would all just rape me and leave my sister alone. I laid there, thought of Tasha, prayed the same thing wasn't happening to her, and wished that she wouldn't hear all the noise and come out of her room. I laid on the floor and didn't pay attention to who was on top of me next. I blocked out everything the guys said. I laid there, stared at the piano, and hoped they would all hurry up and just leave. Someone must have knocked me unconscious because when I opened my eyes, everyone was gone. The house was a mess, and Tasha was nowhere to be found.

I spent the next day cleaning. I was surprised at how sore I felt. Tasha came through the front door. I was so happy to see her. I asked where she had been, and she just looked at me. I wondered if the guys had gotten her too or if she had seen me with all the guys and didn't want anything to do with me like Marie.

I washed the dishes and cleaned the floor. I had no money to replace all the food and knew Mother would be angry. She would think we ate everything; but when my parents came home, they never said a word. Dad never even noticed his gun was missing. I felt so bad about the house and the gun. I washed my parent's sheets and lit a candle in their room on their dresser. I got yelled at for almost catching the house on fire but other than that, nothing.

I walked to school right past Marie's house and saw her out front with another friend, but she ignored me and started talking to her friend. Her friend turned to look at me with disgust. I then realized that rumors about my date with Ron and the entire football team were out, and I was going to have to face Ron. I walked directly to the gym and right up to Ron, but he chuckled and looked at his friends.

I told him, "I want my dad's gun back."

He ignored me and walked off to another workout machine and began lifting weights. I asked over and over until the coach walked up to us and asked what was the problem. I was scared and looked at the floor. The coach held Ron's weight up and looked him in the eyes.

He said, "You take care of her, because if she comes in again it's on you."

Later that day, I walked in the hall and one of the black guys from the football team stopped me and handed me a bag.

"I didn't take it; now you have it so leave us alone."

I felt awkward and thanked him. I was glad to sneak the gun back into my dad's dresser. Tasha never mentioned that night to me — and even years later when I asked her about it, she denied she was even home that night.

Chapter Ten

I hated going to school because I couldn't handle all the remarks and comments from people. They said I was a whore for having sex with the entire football team. I especially feared Tanya who was a thin, pretty girl with blonde hair. She would push my back with her nails and accuse me of giving her boyfriend "the look". I didn't even know who her boyfriend was, but she constantly tried to push me downstairs or run me over with her car on my long walks home from school.

I learned to take the BART to San Francisco to visit my real dad, Dave. He taught me how to ask random people who walked down the street for money.

He said, "If people are dumb enough to give you their money, you are smart enough to take it!"

I gave Dad Dave all the money, but he let me take home a jar of pennies. He used the money for a meal and my BART ticket home. I thought it was fun, like a game of who could get more money.

Dad Dave used the remainder of the money to get massages.

He said the women at the massage place knew him well and really liked him. I sat outside and waited. Dad paid, left a tip, and blew them kisses. The women doing the massages didn't speak any English but seemed fine with my dad — and they were even nice to me. My dad told me that when he would get his massage, he would imagine it was me who gave it to him. I felt like it was creepy, but at least he no longer touched me.

I could never stay at Dad's home in San Francisco. He made it clear that it would not be safe for me to stay the night. So, I would visit for the day, and he would show me his home: a small condominium just off Van Ness Ave. (in San Francisco), a one bedroom, one bathroom with a family room and a tiny kitchen with room for a small table.

"The neighbor's just sold for $599,000 and mine is paid for!" he proudly announced.

I knew he had a great job and worked for the same company for 15 years. He had loyally paid $200 per month child support for my sister and I over the years, which my mother always complained wasn't near enough to support two girls. She would then say it paid for most of their mortgage, and she never had to work. Stepdad John worked six long days a week to provide for us.

So, I thanked my dad and was about to leave when he asked me, "If you ever want to make some real money and give me a massage, I would rather pay you instead of those Asian girls."

I didn't know what to say because I figured the massage would probably be sexual so I just smiled and said, "I'll let you know" and left.

"Some things never change," I thought to myself as I walked to the BART station to go back to Mother's house.

"I sure hope she's not in one of her crazy moods tonight," I muttered aloud.

I took the Bart home, and then hopped on a bus and noticed a roller-skating rink. I had the rest of the money from the panhandling as we had collected more than usual — and I had some left even after the food, massage, BART and bus ride. I probably had enough to roller skate so I got off the bus and went inside the building. I paid my fee and rented skates. It was my first time roller skating. I had such a great time that I started going every Sunday evening and even invited Tasha.

We had to be extra nice to Mother so she wouldn't put us on restriction. Mother used the fact that we liked to roller skate as an excuse to make us do extra chores and things to help her around the house. Mother was doing really well and seemed happier. She got a job grooming dogs, which gave her a chance to leave the house once in a while. She was really proud of how good she was at doing it, too.

Tasha and I took the bus to the skating rink and had to leave before the last bus at night. One night at the roller rink, I met a girl named Tina. She was a few years older and had her own car. She lived in Hayward and said she could give me rides, and we could go to the roller rink together. She was tall and thin with green eyes and freckles on her face. She made me feel safe when girls from my school would stare at me or make comments about my sexuality or being a whore. Tina taught me to just enjoy the music and forget about everything and everyone else. I didn't know then what I know now: Tina would become my best friend, and she would be a part of my life for the rest of my life.

My sister and I spent more and more time together. Mother was working. We were home alone and went to the creek to discover animals. We made steps out of the hillside to make it easier to climb down to the water's edge to catch frogs.

One day Tasha thought it would be funny to push me into the creek water. She laughed until she saw the fear on my face. I couldn't swim, and then she couldn't reach me because the sides of the creek were so slippery and muddy. She found a stick and tried to get me to grab at it. I couldn't reach and panicked when a large snake swam near me. I screamed, and then I saw Dad run down the steps toward me. He jumped in the creek, grabbed me, and pulled me out as he continually slipped back in the creek water.

It was something we all decided not to tell Mother, but our little brother Jeremy accidently mentioned it that night at dinner. Mother put us both on restriction for the creek incident. Later on, Tasha knocked at her closet door, and I knocked back. After our parents went to bed, Tasha was outside my bedroom window.

I opened the window, and Tasha whispered, "Get ready and meet us out front."

I got ready as fast as I could and snuck out the window, went around the side of the house, and met my sister and Tina out front. We got in Tina's car and drove off to the roller rink. We had a great time until I saw Tanya skate right past me hand-in-hand with a tall skinny guy with greasy blonde hair, acne, and a large comb in his back pocket.

I told Tasha and Tina that was the girl who had harassed me at school. Tanya went into the bathroom, and Tasha followed her. Tina and I stayed at the roller-rink food court in line to order Cherry ICEE's while we gazed at the bathroom. Finally, we saw Tasha come out all wet with a big grin on her face. She skated up to the food court and sat at a table. She stared at the bathroom door. We got our ICEE's and joined her.

"What happened, Tasha?" I asked.

"Nothing. She won't be bothering you anymore."

Tanya slowly skated out of the bathroom and held her hair with her hands. Her hair was soaked.

I looked at Tasha, "You didn't?"

"Oh yeah," Tasha replied, "she's not going to harass my little sister anymore."

We all laughed as Tanya went to collect her purse and her boyfriend as she skated past us to leave. Tanya never said anything to me at school again, but she always smirked, stared, and whispered to her friends as if she were talking bad about me.

I hated school. I had no friends and my sister had started going to a different school because of her modeling career. Mother put her in an adult high school in another town that allowed her to take time off as needed for her modeling jobs.

She had already been in several commercials and played body double for a famous actress. Mother purchased a BMW and groomed dogs to make the payments so Tasha could have the model look and appear successful. Mother was also busy volunteering for hospice.

Chapter Eleven

Mother stood in the hallway that separated our rooms and in a gentle voice, asked me and my sister to sit at the kitchen table to talk. She looked very serious and seemed concerned. We walked down the hall to the kitchen and sat at the kitchen table.

She said, "I have been having horrible nightmares and just can't sleep. I had another dream last night that I sleepwalked into your rooms while you were asleep and stabbed you both with a knife, killing you." She paused and added, "So for your protection I am installing locks on the inside of your doors so you can feel safe. Today we have a fresh start."

She cheered up, smiled, and continued to tell us, "There is a war in another country, but don't worry because I have plans that if a war were to break out here, I would poison your food, and you would both fall asleep fast!" She looked at the plate of food that sat on the kitchen table and screamed, "Now, eat your food!"

We looked at the table and noticed tuna sandwiches cut up on a plate. We looked at each other. Without a word that our sandwiches might be poisoned and thoughts that Mother just wanted to get rid of us, we numbly ate. We stared at her. She was overly interested that we eat our sandwiches. We just knew something was wrong, but we also realized we had no choice.

Mother was in a strange mood. She looked silly like she was up to no good. She couldn't sit still and fidgeted in her seat. She began to chuckle as we ate, asked us if the sandwiches were good, and tried hard not to laugh. There was lots of mayonnaise and lettuce, it wasn't bad just dry, even with all the mayonnaise. I looked at my sister's face. She stared at the counter and started spitting the food out into her napkin. I looked on the counter and noticed two open and empty cans of cat food.

Mother began cracking up, laughing, and glaring at me with an angry face.

She yelled, "Finish it!" which I did, slowly.

My sister got up and ran to the bathroom. I heard a scream. Mother sat patiently as she watched me eat. She told me she was visiting a hospice client who had cancer. She was too old and tired to take care of her old cat. Mother took the old cat and its food and told the sweet old lady that she knew a place to take the cat — a place where there was plenty of room for the cat to roam. She described a beautiful stream with lots of shade trees, blue skies, and a waterfall that created a rainbow. Mother got up from her chair, started dancing around, and sang, "heaven".

I felt sick and ran to the bathroom. My sister stopped and warned me not to go in there, but I ran inside. I sat over the toilet and threw up cat food while I cried. I looked into the tub and saw the old cat in the tub filled with water, floating lifeless. I knew Mother had done this thinking it was funny. I sat on the floor, hung onto the toilet bowl, and felt dizzy and sick to my stomach. I knew that I had to get the courage to take out the cat and clean the bathtub before Mother got anymore crazy ideas.

After that horrendous meal, Mother did put the locks on our doors. I stayed in my room almost all day and night. Mother did not notice I hadn't gone to school or even the roller rink. I suffered from depression although I didn't know it at that time. I just didn't want to leave my room or even unlock the door. Mother was gone a lot, and when she was home she was busy babysitting kids so she could save money to buy my sister a nose job. She didn't like the way Tasha's nostrils were getting large and round. She said she had a black person's nose and wouldn't make many movies unless she changed it.

So, Mother took Tasha to a surgeon and started to save. Tasha didn't make enough with her modeling money to pay for the BMW sports car and nose job so Mother had the BMW payments subtracted monthly from Dad's checking account. She got the statement and made me carefully whiteout the automatic payment, and then add it up to make it appear it was a smaller fee for something else. I was good at doing it, too. My hand technique was slow and steady. I was afraid to think what would happen if I made an error.

Mother gave me a break from cleaning the house and wanted me to see the volunteer work she did for hospice. She said there was a neighbor down the street who was on hospice and dying from cancer. We walked just a few doors down, and Mrs. Jones opened the door. She looked shocked to have company, but let us in. Although I remembered her from walking me to school years earlier and showing me my classroom, she didn't recognize me. She looked at me, and for a moment I thought she would recall our first meeting, but instead she took my hand and led me to the kitchen. She looked out the window.

Mrs. Jones put her finger to her lips and said, "Shhhh, do you hear it? It's the ice-cream man."

She began to dance around to music that was only in her head.

Mother looked at me and said, "You think I'm crazy."

Mother began to go through Mrs. Jones' drawers and closets taking a few items and reminding her she wouldn't need them, but I think Mrs. Jones didn't even notice. Mother stuffed the items in her purse, and we walked home. We left Mrs. Jones alone in her kitchen to dance.

Chapter Twelve

Tasha was in bed. She was in terrible pain as she recovered from her "nasal reconstructive job," as Mother called it. Mother knocked briskly at my bedroom door. I rushed to open it, and Mother seemed overwhelmed with joy as she began to tell me that she had a vision. She declared she was psychic. She thought Tasha was going to be a huge star but needed to have breast implants. Mother was so thrilled to hear about this new form of plastic surgery. I looked at mother and wondered how many surgeries she was going to make Tasha go through when she interrupted my thoughts.

"I am certain she will get more commercials and modeling jobs," Mother declared. "We just have to do this because this is something Tasha really needs!"

Tasha heard us and moaned from her room, "I need my pain medicine, I can't do this again. I don't want big boobs!"

Going to Tasha's bedside, Mother screamed, "You are not taking any more of that damn medication, you are not the one sick here. I am! So stop your complaining."

I knew Tasha was in pain. When Mother went to lie down on her bed, I heard her switch on the television. It was her favorite show where this black lady interviewed white people, so I knew Mother would be glued to that show for about an hour. I quietly went to look for Tasha's medication, but all I found was an empty bottle.

I walked over to Mrs. Jones' house and knocked at the door. I hoped she would remember me. She answered the door. I asked her for aspirin, and she let me in the house, but I wasn't sure what pills to take. Just then Mr. Jones walked in the door as I searched one of her drawers. He seemed appropriately shocked to see me. He was a tall, thin man with gray hair and looked nice but tired. I introduced myself and let him know that my sister had just had surgery, and I couldn't get a hold of my mother.

"She's in pain and needs medication," I explained.

Mr. Jones left for a moment and returned with a bottle of pills. He said to give her two every four hours and wished me luck. I thanked him and left.

My sister continued to cry and complain about the pain. Mother had a psychic premonition and decided that Tasha was possessed. She knew of a woman named Maryanne who performed satanic rituals. Mother told us we were to go with her that evening to get rid of the demons. I later helped Mother carry Tasha to the car, and we drove for over an hour. It was dark when we showed up at the old, small house in a neighborhood without curbs or streetlights. We carried Tasha into the house, and a group of women who were all wearing black waited for us. The house was dark with several candles lit. The woman named Maryanne greeted us then demanded that I go back and wait in the car. It must have taken hours, but Mother finally walked out of the house and carried Tasha.

Mother kept repeating "sorry" over and over to Tasha. Tasha was naked with only a blanket covering her. I stayed with her in the backseat and held her as Mother drove us home. She told me all about her out-of-body experience.

"I really am a psychic, tonight I proved that," she bragged.

Not long after Tasha recovered from her nose job, she also got a new procedure done — breast augmentation. Doctors placed silicone bags into incisions under her breasts. I was home that day just sitting in my room, spending my day with Timmy, my parakeet, and waiting for mother and Tasha to return. Mother came storming into the house. She was angry and slammed the door behind her.

"Where's Tasha?" I asked.

"That selfish, unappreciative bitch wanted me to drive home!" yelled Mother. "How dare she! I was the one up all night. I am the one who doesn't feel well. She expects me to pay for her surgery, take her to her surgery, and then drive her home like I am some sort of chauffer!"

Mother was angry, pouted to her room, and slammed the door. I waited by the window for Tasha. The BMW pulled up in the driveway. I was shocked to notice Tasha had driven home herself just after her surgery. I went to help her out of her car and into her room to lay her on her bed. She cried and told me how she and Mother got in a fight about driving — and that the nurse even told Mother that she couldn't drive home.

"Where's your pain medication?" I asked.

"Mother took it," she replied.

I went into the kitchen and saw an empty bag. I knew Mother had it. Instead of upsetting Mother, I walked over to Mrs. Jones' house and knocked on the door. It took awhile for Mr. Jones to answer but he finally did. I noticed he was crying so much he could hardly talk.

"I need more pain medication for my sister," I asked and looked at him with concern.

He didn't answer but let me in the house. He put together a bag of medicines and said to flush what we don't use.

I said, "Doesn't Mrs. Jones need these?"

He looked surprised as he continued to cry and said, "Didn't your mother tell you? Mrs. Jones passed away last night. Your mother was here. She passed away peacefully in your mother's arms. Thank God your mother was here, she's such an angel."

I rushed home angry at Mother. I thought this was why she was so tired and couldn't drive my sister. Why didn't she tell us about Mrs. Jones? I took the medicine and a tall glass of water to my sister and told her about Mrs. Jones. I looked up and noticed Mother in the doorway — her face looked green and her eyes had an angry look as she squinted them.

She said, "Now you know what I have to do volunteering for hospice: I have to witness death. Mrs. Jones wasn't willing to die. She put up a big fight. But, she was too weak. She asked me why I lifted her nightgown and pulled down her panties to insert a pill up her rectum. I told her she was constipated, and I was trying to help her; but really, I played God and gave her a black-death pill. It didn't take as long as the rest to stop her from fighting me. I held her down as she stopped breathing. I felt her last breath while she looked into my eyes."

I got so angry, lunged, and threw Mother on the hall floor. I held her down with all my weight, and I began punching her in her face, neck and chest. I took her head with my hands and began to pound her head against the floor with all my strength. For the first time in years, Dad came home early from work and opened the front door. He stared at me for a second and dropped his lunchbox to the floor. I saw anger in his face as he dashed for me. So as fast as I could, I got off Mother, turned around, and ran into my bedroom where I slammed the door and held it with all my weight as I locked it. I pulled the small dresser in front of the door to give it extra strength as Dad kicked and punched the door as he tried to knock it down.

He yelled, "You better open this door!"

Hours passed, and I heard a lot of talking in the kitchen. Dad had decided to call the police, and they were writing a report. Dad was still angry, and Tasha was knocked out in her bed from medication. The police insisted I open my door, which I did. They informed me that they were removing me from my home and to pack a bag of clothes. I asked my dad if I could also take Timmy my parakeet and he said yes. Dad would not look me in the eyes, but he did say, "Get out of my house," as I left with my bag of clothes, my parakeet, and two police officers. I noticed the nicer of the two police officers had a name badge, "Stanley". He was calm and talked to me to let me know that we were headed to the station to find me a place to stay.

Chapter Thirteen

Stanley had called the few people I could think of who might let me stay. My real father said it was not an option, and I couldn't agree more. The other option was a friend of Stanley's named Camille. She was Mormon, had six kids, and could use some help. I was surprised when she agreed on the phone to allow me to stay at her house even though she had not met me.

Stanley took me to her house; it was a huge two-story mansion with a large, well-manicured lawn. She opened the tall front door. I noticed her large smile with red lipstick and her twinkling eyes with lots of blue eye shadow. She showed me in, and Stanley wished me well. I got my own room away from the others, downstairs with a bathroom next to it. There was a mattress on the floor and a dresser against a wall.

She smiled and said, "Stay as long as you like."

I couldn't believe she was so nice. The first night, I met the kids and we sat at the dining-room table. Camille served our dinner. The kids told me it was family game night, but I was so tired I decided to sleep, and I did go right to bed. Camille said

I slept for two days.

"You must have needed it," she said and smiled when I finally returned to life.

Camille never asked about my story nor did she ask about what happened or anything. She worked on my school enrollment and had trouble figuring out my grade level. I had to take a test — and that's when Camille realized I couldn't read. She quickly took action and spent all summer teaching me to read. She drew pictures and explained the *Book of Mormon* to me. I enjoyed reading, going to church, and playing with the other kids on family game night. I loved playing with the kids.

High school was a short walk from the house. I had a hard time adjusting to my schedule and getting to school on time. Driver's education was first period. Camille reminded me that I would never drive if I didn't pass that class so I made an effort. I also got my first A in drama that year. My drama teacher said he never gave out A's but I had one. I couldn't perform in any of the school plays or join the baseball teams because I needed parental consent, and Mother told Camille I didn't deserve it.

Christmas was beautiful with a huge tree, and I even got a gift from Santa. Camille handed it to me, and I held it.

She said, "Open it!" so I did.

It was a wrinkled pair of pants. I thanked her and jumped up to give her a hug. She laughed and couldn't believe how happy I was to get maternity pants (it was supposed to be a joke).

"Your gift card is under those old pants!" said Camille.

I was fine with the old pants, but also was excited to shop

for something new for myself.

"I don't remember when the last time was that I even went into a store," I told Camille.

She smiled and gave me a hug.

She said, "Your mother dropped off a gift, too," she said and handed me a neatly wrapped gift.

I sat and stared at it as I slowly opened it; it was a pink robe and a fluffy stuffed bear. I told Camille I didn't want it, but she convinced me to use it so I did.

I had finished my junior year with a 2.5 grade point average, which was the best accomplishment I ever made. Most of my grades were D's except drama in which I got an A. Camille had bad news to share with me. Her husband's company was being relocated to Utah, and she had spoken to my mother and asked her to sign and allow me to go, but she had refused.

"There's more — she wants custody of you. Social services is allowing her to begin visitation tomorrow — and because you are not yet 18 and still in school, your mother still has her rights."

"What about my rights?" I demanded.

"You're a minor and still in school," reminded Camille.

"Try the visitations; see if you can talk your mother into letting you move with us. Our door is always open to you. You just have to get your mother to sign."

Camille gave me a sincere smile and a pat on the back.

Mother showed up right on time for visitation. She looked nice with a shorter haircut (although her hair had more gray), she even dressed like she had a job interview and wore a nice dark-blue pantsuit. She watched the tricks I taught Timmy my parakeet and told me how much everyone missed me. She seemed really nervous to be alone with me in my new room and her hands shook. She said things had really changed, and that she took psychic classes. She was convinced that her vision was to have me home. I told her how great I was doing in school, and Mother reminded me that school was another reason for me to stay in California.

"You can't just stop school before your senior year and expect things to be the same in a different state; plus, I am not sure I agree with the Mormon religion. You know those Mormons have to go door-to-door, knock, and meet strangers — and that can be dangerous," she said.

Mother sounded concerned and sincere, and I agreed to move home. I didn't feel like I had much of a choice. I hoped things would be different, but was I wrong.

Chapter Fourteen

Camille let me stay until the day the movers came to move them. It took two extra-large trucks and four guys. We had already packed all the clothes and decorations so they were ready to go, but the movers had to wrap and carry out all the furniture. All my things were already at Mother's house except for a bag of clothes. I spent the next several hours in the backyard with the kids. We jumped on the trampoline and played chase as we waited for the movers to finish so I could say goodbye and move home. I wanted to run and jump on that last moving truck as I watched it drive out of sight, but I knew I had no choice but to go back home.

I walked the five miles across town with my bag of clothes and cried. I felt confused and upset to have to go back and dreaded each step as I got closer to that house. Just the previous week Mother and I had a visit, and we had an argument because Mother told me that Tasha had gotten married, and when I asked why no one told me and why I wasn't invited to the wedding, Mother had replied not to worry.

"Only close family and friends were invited," she said.

I got angry with her. So she left, and we hadn't spoken since. I was happy to hear Tasha had met someone and was able to move out of the house. I was shocked when I arrived at Mother's house because all my things were on the front lawn including Timmy, my parakeet. It all sat under a shade tree for me. I went to the door, and it was locked. I knocked because I didn't have a key.

Dad answered and said, "Mother is sick and didn't want to be the one to tell you but she's upset and concerned to let you move back home. She's afraid of you, Jen, and frankly, I don't blame her."

He looked down at the ground and then back at me and continued, "You can't stay here."

He closed the door, and I stood there and wondered where I could possibly go. I couldn't think straight — I was an empty shell. I only had one friend so I took what I could carry, my bag of clothes and my parakeet cage, and walked to the bus.

When I arrived at my old friend Tina's house she told me I could stay the night until we figured out where I could go. We went for a walk to a nearby market and noticed police everywhere; we heard that someone had just kidnapped a girl who was in the store when she walked out to get her scooter. We were shocked that we happened to be there right after something so scary happened to another girl. Tina said it was a good thing it wasn't us, but I thought at least I would have somewhere to live. That night it was all over the news, the girl was only 12, her mother was crying and begging whoever grabbed her to return her. Tina's mother was glued to the TV all night crying and praying for the safe return of that young girl.

Tina had found a friend of a friend who said I could live with her for a while. She lived in the San Francisco Bay Area and had her own apartment. She was 23 with long, blonde, curly hair and a large-framed tanned body. She spoke slowly and seemed like maybe she was on a lot of medication or something. Her name was Ann, and she seemed nice. She explained that I could stay for a few months to get on my feet, but there was only one room and one bed so we had to share. Ann made it very clear that she worked from home and on weekends. I would have to find another place to stay, but only on the weekends.

I asked what she did for a living, and she looked surprised that I asked.

She answered, "I give massages on the weekends, and I have a lot of clients so they wait in the family room on the sofa all day and night. I use my bed to give them massages. During the week, I sell medication so someone is always knocking at the door around the clock — that's how I pay my bills."

I was surprised that she was a professional businesswoman — and I admired that.

Living with Ann was fun but tiring. She always got money and gifts from her clients, and she bought a lot of clothes, which she shared with me. I even got a job as a waitress and worked as much as I could. It was across town so I walked a lot and took two buses. Tina picked me up every Friday night after the restaurant I worked in closed, and we went out dancing in local bars. I just used her identification. I waited several minutes for her to go in with her driver's license, and then I would show them mine. We really looked nothing alike but somehow, it worked. We danced until the bars closed. Weekend after weekend, we looked forward to dancing and the after-parties. We stayed out all night.

One night, I stood under an air-conditioning pipe. I took a break from dancing when a really good-looking, tall guy not much older than me, came up and pointed up at the pipe that was slowly dripping condensation on my head. He laughed and said it was sweat from too many people in one place. He said his name was Michael. He looked like prince charming from a book I once saw in a classroom. He had a tan face, with dark curly hair, and he dressed great with denim blue jeans, snakeskin boots, a T-shirt, and a jean jacket. His eyes were hazel green, and he looked at me in a way no other guy ever had, like he really liked me. Michael had the nicest teeth I had ever seen and a perfect smile. I grabbed Michael's arm, and we went to the dance floor.

We danced for hours, laughed, and yelled at each other over the loud music. I went home with Michael that night and stayed the rest of the weekend with him.

Tina had picked me up Tuesday morning from Michael's two-story house that he and a roommate rented. She took me to Ann's place. I realized I had not taken my birth control pills for four days and took all four with a large glass of water as soon as I returned to Ann's apartment.

Weekdays went by fast as I worked in the busy restaurant. Ann also had company in and out during the weekdays to pick up drugs. Turns out the "medication" Ann sold was crank. Ann taught me all about crank. She made it right in her kitchen and sold it to clients who showed up all day and night at the door for pick up and deliveries; but Ann would not let me try it. She just asked for my help with the clients. In exchange for helping her with her side business, I didn't have to pay her rent and could save to move out.

Weekends were all about going to bars, watching bands play, and hanging out with Michael after he got off work. I always looked forward to seeing Michael. I thought about him all week, which put a smile on my face. After a few months, I started to feel sick and couldn't get the energy after work to go out with Tina to the bars; but Ann wouldn't let me stay at her place either on weekends so I called Michael, and he let me stay with him.

Michael was a male dancer and left me at his place while he went out to work. I was so sick. I ended up staying a week at Michael's place and called in sick at the restaurant. One night, Michael didn't come home. He didn't return his pages so I called Tina to pick me up. As I waited for her, Michael's roommate Steve came in the door.

He looked exhausted and, in tears, said, "Isn't it sad about Michael?"

I looked at him funny.

"You don't know?"

I looked shocked and shook my head.

"Michael got into a car accident the other night," explained Steve. "I thought someone had called you? He had been drinking, said he was in a hurry, and had to get home. We tried to stop him but couldn't. We heard the ambulance shortly after and went to see if it was Michael; it was him. He had drifted off the side of the road and crashed into a pole. At first, we thought he would be all right but hours later the doctor announced he died."

Tina arrived and waited for me. I was so upset that I had run to the kitchen sink to throw up. Steve was too upset to say goodbye as we left. I knew he was tired and had been up all night dealing with his best friend and roommate's death.

Chapter Fifteen

"Are you pregnant?" Tina asked.

I looked at her in shock, "No."

"Are you sure? You're always tired and throwing up. When was your last period?"

"I don't know, but I have been on the pill for a year and don't have them each month. Plus, I have only been with Michael."

Thinking back about the weekend we met and how I forgot to take the pills for four days made me wonder. I began to think about how I had been sick and my jeans and shoes felt tight. I was getting teased at the restaurant for soaking my hamburgers in too much ketchup, and Ann had been upset with me a lot for being too tired to answer the door for clients.

"There's no way."

But truth was, I was pregnant — no doubt about that one.

I confirmed that I was already five months pregnant at the teen pregnancy clinic. I decided to visit Mother since Ann said it was time for me to move out — that a baby had no business in her home — and I agreed.

I took a bus and went to the place where my godmother Sherry had told me Mother groomed dogs. She was busy, but I insisted so she rolled her eyes, dropped the brush she used to groom a dog, and stopped to talk to me. We sat down on the curb just outside the grooming center. I told her I had something to tell her but wanted her to guess. She asked if I had AIDS or cancer (she looked excited at this idea). I told her I was pregnant.

She rolled her eyes and said, "Oh, that's nothing. Just have an abortion."

I told her I was due in a few months, and I told her about Michael. Mother decided I had no choice but to give the baby up for adoption since there was no father. I never objected or questioned her. I decided to keep the baby and things would just have to work out.

I stayed at Tina's house for a few days. I had to find somewhere to live, so I made up a fake application and I applied at an apartment. I even made up a fake career and hoped they wouldn't check. Lucky for me, in those days there were no computers and no cell phones so the landlord accepted my application. I gave her the first month's rent and deposit from the tips I had saved from the restaurant. I was able to immediately move into the downstairs unit. I didn't care that I had nothing and slept on the floor, but Mother and several of her friends collected things and my apartment began to look decent. I got a job at an insurance company and began to learn to process medical claims. I even qualified for medical insurance.

Things went well except for continual calls from some couple — they harassed me and claimed Mother told them that they were going to adopt my baby. The woman had already had a baby shower. They insisted I tell them my due date. I argued with them and told them not to call my work; my baby was not available for adoption. Employees at work soon got word that I was expecting and threw me my own baby shower. Mother also bought baby gifts from her favorite thrift store once she was finally convinced that the baby wasn't going up for adoption and I planned to keep him. Mother had convinced me and everyone else that I was having a girl even though the sonogram clearly showed it was a boy. Mother had a psychic premonition that it was a girl, and all the gifts mother bought me were pink.

The same day I received notice that the company I worked for was going to lay me off (my position was no longer available) was also the same day I went into labor. Mother, Tina, and my godmother Sherry all showed up at the hospital. Sherry had been the one helping me to get my apartment ready for the baby. She had collected a crib, rocking chair, and used clothes. Mother convinced me not to put the baby's father Michael on the birth certificate because if I ever found a man who would marry me, it would make it easier to just say he's the father and add him. Although I agreed, I later regretted this decision because I was unable to collect social security support for our baby.

Sherry was so excited. She normally dressed fancy so I was surprised to see her wear a sweat suit, but it was a bright, shiny purple with pink flowers. She had really long eyelashes and bright purple eye shadow and puffy blonde hair. She was about my mother's age of 40. I loved to watch her face shrivel up as she squeezed my hand and squealed enthusiastically, "Pushhh." The doctor kept reminding her not to tell me that, yet. I decided to use Sherry's bright pink flowers on her sweat suit as my focal point.

Tina came back into the room (she had been there and left) and asked to speak to the doctor. Then she left the room with him. Meanwhile, Mother told me that she read that if you masturbate prior to the baby's birth, giving birth would be the best orgasm a woman would ever have. I got scared and thought, I never had an orgasm but the contractions in no way, shape or form felt good. I began to feel scared and tightened up terrified to give birth. The doctor came back into the room and asked to speak to my mother. As they walked out together, I asked Tina what that was all about, but she wouldn't tell me. Turned out that Mother had invited the couple who wanted to adopt my baby to wait in the waiting room in case I changed my mind, but the doctor made them leave.

Two long days passed of hard labor and on April 1987, Matthew was born. He was the most beautiful baby I had ever seen with dark skin and blonde hair — and did he cry! I was able to hold him for just a minute, but the pediatrician had to take him immediately away as he had forced trauma to his head and a 104-degree fever. They told me they were unable to circumcise Matthew, which was fine with me. No one would ever touch my baby's penis, not even me.

Tasha remarkably never showed up to see the baby. I questioned Mother why Tasha had not come to see the baby. She told me that Tasha was hurt that I was having a baby before her. She was the older one and even got married and had a husband. She felt she was the one who should be having the baby. I felt hurt for Tasha. I wished she would have been the one to have the first baby, too.

Chapter Sixteen

Matthew was such a cute baby, and I adored him. Every single moment I just didn't want to take my eyes off him. He kept me so busy that I was actually glad I had lost my job because I knew I couldn't leave him to go to work. Matthew looked like he could be Tasha's baby with tan skin and blonde curly hair. I was working hard on his baby book, filling out all the important details, including when he rolled, crawled, walked, and how much he had grown.

I nursed him his first three years. The doctors said it was great that I had nursed for three years because Matthew was 90 percent for his height and 50 percent for his weight, which meant he was healthy. The doctor suggested I wean Matthew off from nursing. So I went home and started giving Matthew a bottle. I wasn't working, and I qualified for a low-income milk and cereal program that really helped me learn about nutrition. Matthew and I were inseparable, and he became the best thing that ever happened to me. Although we didn't have much money, I found babysitting and house-cleaning jobs, and things just seemed to work out.

Years went by fast as I took care of Matthew. On his third birthday, Tasha was excited to throw Matthew a birthday party. Her husband Richard rented a super-hero costume, and he planned to jump over the back-porch fence to surprise the kids. I felt bad for Tasha and Richard because they had been trying to have a baby; they even had the baby room all set up with a Mickey Mouse theme. Each month Tasha would call me and ask how Matthew was doing. I always knew she had her period and felt sad. My best friend Marie from my elementary school days had come with her son (we reconnected). She had also gotten pregnant by her first boyfriend but was now raising her son Kevin as a single mother, too. Marie's mother was disappointed but still helped Marie with the baby so she could continue her education. During the party Tasha told me she was concerned that I still hadn't potty trained Matthew, and after the party she stayed a few days to work with him to potty train.

The party was great; several kids from our apartment complex showed up for hotdogs, cake, and a super-hero surprise. Tasha stayed and as I cleaned up, she took Matthew to the bathroom to help him and yelled for me to come see his penis. I ran into the bathroom and was surprised to see Matthew's penis looked purple and puffy. Tasha said we needed to rush Matthew to the hospital as his penis looked infected.

Tasha and I spent the entire night in the hospital waiting room. Matthew had to have an emergency circumcision due to the fact that I was not pulling the skin back and cleaning it. I felt so awful and cried all night while my baby suffered because of me. I never touched or even looked at his penis even when I changed his diapers because I felt uncomfortable and didn't know I was supposed to do it.

As hours passed Tasha and I sat and talked about our past. I asked her why we never celebrated her birthday and she said, "I was born in September, 1964 on the only day that Mother did not want to give birth. That is the same day as our Grandmother Ruth's birthday. Mother hated her mother; she was always talking about the awful things her mother did to her."

Tasha looked at me and continued, "Grandma abused mother sexually for years. Mother said she was a prostitute and sold her body to pay their bills. Sometimes when the men would see Mother they would ask Ruth how much, and she sold our mother to these guys. Mother would have to do whatever they said or her mother would beat her. Ruth told mother that it was her fault that men found her attractive because of the way Mother 'flirted' with them, and she deserved it."

I asked Tasha about Keith, the guy who Mother had allowed to photograph Tasha and take her places alone.

"Whatever happened to him after they found you in that hotel room?"

Tasha looked down at the ground and began to cry but put her hand up as if to stop me from the hug I wanted to give her.

"Keith tied me up to a hotel room bed and raped me several times a day. I was so scared because he had a gun and threatened to kill me. I didn't want to die so I just lay there scared for my life and disgusted to have this older man force me to have sex with him. He kept trying to make me tell him that I liked it, and he wanted me to smile and participate in his sexual fantasies. I watched his porn tapes over and over. He told me that he knew I wanted him because of the way I dressed. He said I wore bathing suits because I wanted to attract men and have sex. He said all men think like that. Men see a girl who is just trying to look like the women in magazines who dress pretty with short skirts and makeup, and men think they are doing it to attract them because we want to have sex ... sick!"

She paused and continued, "So after you moved, things got worse for me because the police wanted me to testify, but Mother said that it wasn't his fault. He convinced Mother that he had never done anything like that before, and he would never do anything like that again. He said he really cared about our family and didn't want my friends and the whole world to know about what I went through because it would ruin my reputation, no one would want to be my friend, and I wouldn't get any jobs. So Mother agreed to drop the charges, but told him to stay away from me."

I asked if she had agreed with that decision.

She said, "Well, I did but I came to regret it."

"What happened, Tasha?" I asked.

"Keith was later charged and convicted of molesting other girls, some as young as eight-years old. He had signed up as a volunteer softball coach for girls, and some of the parents would just drop off their kids. They trusted Keith because he was such a nice guy. He was sentenced to prison and committed suicide before he served. I just feel like if I would have followed through, maybe I could have prevented some of those girls from going through what I once experienced. These girls will never be the same. Thank God you have a boy."

"Yes," I agreed.

Mother really didn't come around a whole lot, but she did stop by the week before my birthday. She told me how I was going to have to get someone to watch Matthew. She was taking me to a Halloween party and was making my costume as my birthday gift.

"By the way, if Dad asks, I am paying your rent," said Mother, who was serious and smiled.

She held Matthew on her lap and looked happy to see him, and he was excited to have company.

"What are you really doing with the money?" I asked Mother. "I have to help your sister; she's leaving Richard. He's been so controlling, and she needs to get back on her feet so I am helping her get back into modeling. She deserves new clothes and a new car. She needs to look for a place to rent, too."

I looked down at the same green stretch pants and matching sweat shirt I always wore and said, "She can stay here and help me with Matthew so I can go back to school. I really want to finish high school and get a good job."

Mother laughed, "Now what do you think you could possibly do to support you and Matthew? I know you need to meet a guy and get pregnant so he'll marry you! Maybe at the Halloween party, you'll meet someone."

My godmother Sherry watched Matthew, and for the first time I left him so I could attend the Halloween party with Mother. Sherry said not to worry and have a great time and that she would take Matthew out for a walk to stop him from crying when I left. Mother made me a waitress costume, and I really thought I looked good.

She also had a surprise for me and said, "Ron. Remember him from high school? You had that big crush on him?"

I was shocked and embarrassed, but Ron seemed nice and happy to see me. I had been lonely taking care of Matthew. Ron sat with me for hours. He told me how bad he felt that his friends had raped me and taken the gun. He convinced me he had nothing to do with it, and he didn't even know they would go that night. The evening went by, and I felt drunk and tired and began to look for my mother. The house was dark and decorated for Halloween. I looked all over the house and realized that Mother had left me there alone with Ron. Ron pulled me by my arm into the back bedroom. I passed out on the bed from all the drinking. I woke up naked on the bed and alone in a strange room in an unfamiliar house. I walked home for miles dressed like a waitress with torn fishnet stockings and heels that killed my feet.

Later on, I hoped to hear from him. I told Tina all about him.

"Have you heard from him?" Tina asked one afternoon.

She patiently waited for an answer I knew she had already guessed.

"No, okay!" I barked back at her.

"It has been months, and you're acting the way you did when you were pregnant with Matthew," she spat.

"Oh no," I thought.

I hadn't even considered it, but she was right. I knew I was pregnant again. I sat on my brown Goodwill couch that was pushed against a wall in my apartment and stared at her as I began to cry. Tina was so tall and thin with long, straight hair. She wore Levis jeans and t-shirts. She was also tough. She wouldn't put up with anyone mistreating her. I don't even think anyone had ever done so. She didn't date much. She was picky.

"I'm 22, and I can't afford another kid," I lamented. "I have no choice but to abort."

I looked over at Mathew and realized I had just had this conversation with him listening in. It brought back memories of my mother when she talked to my stepfather about aborting my brother Jeremy. I remembered how much that conversation had affected me and my sister. I quickly changed my mind.

I said, "I am having another baby, and Matthew is going to have a brother to play with."

Tina rolled her eyes as she had had enough. She grabbed her purse, and on her way out she turned to look at me and said, "You are never going to get off welfare."

Her look told me she had given up on me, but I knew she was not going to be angry forever.

Chapter Seventeen

"Thank God!" I announced during my sonogram with my second son, Cole. "After promising Matthew a brother to play with, it is a boy!"

I was so excited just thinking of the two boys growing up together and being best friends. I had daydreamed about raising my two boys and all the fun times we would have as a happy little family. Walks in the park, bus rides to the city. I was going to be the best mom ever!

The pregnancy was different because there was a living father, but he chose not to be included. There was no baby shower or gifts, but I had the things I kept from Matthew, which wasn't much, but I knew it would have to do. I planned on nursing and tried to find programs to allow me to continue my education. I had visions of being a businesswoman who dressed up in suits and high heels. I wanted to stand tall and have people look at me. I wanted them to admire me the same way Mother stared and admired the black lady who interviewed movie stars on television. I knew there was more out there for me, and I also knew that Mother was right: I was a 22-year-old, uneducated mother of two on welfare. Who would want me now? I had no choice but to raise my children alone and find a way to go back to school.

Cole came quickly on Valentine's Day, the fastest, quickest labor ever the nurse said after he was born. When I got to the hospital, the nurse told me that just because I was due didn't mean he would be born the exact due date. She had me lay down in a room as she checked me in, and said I wasn't even dilated. I insisted he was coming as she left the room and later returned to find me pushing. Thank God she came back to check on me. Cole slipped right out; the doctor had to cut me to avoid tearing as my new son was in a hurry to get into the world.

Mother came to visit and even Ron stopped by to hold him, but I spent the night and the following day alone with no visitors and drove home alone with my new baby. An apartment neighbor was so kind to watch Matthew while I was gone. I was more excited to see him and introduce him to his new baby brother Cole. Cole was very pale with dark eyes and orange hair that stuck straight out on each side and on top.

Matthew looked sad and said, "I wanted a brother to play with. When is he going to play with me, Mommy?"

I looked at Matthew's sweet, innocent face and reminded him that he would grow each day and one day be big enough to play. Matthew smiled and ran to his room to play with the super-hero action figures that my godmother Sherry had bought him. Sherry knew I could hardly afford my rent on welfare and had been doing anything I could to make up the difference by babysitting and cleaning houses. I don't know if I ever thanked her enough for all her help with my first child.

Later I called Tasha with good news, "I finally got approved on the low-income rental list to move to an affordable apartment!"

Tasha seemed happy for me but was busy getting in shape. I could hear her puffing as she spoke.

"That's great, Jen. I have been so busy working out so I'll look perfect when I body double for Sarah Lee. I get to do all the nudity parts and all the running, jumping, and anything else that she won't."

I was excited for Tasha; she was always so lucky to have such a great body, but I also knew how badly she wanted a baby and decided not to talk about my kids to her.

"You know, Jen, I would help you if I could but I have to get my body in perfect condition so when they call, I'll be ready!"

"I understand. Love you," I said as I hung up, grabbed Matthew and Cole, the diaper bag, and walked to the old orange car my godmother Sherry allowed me to use as I made low monthly payments to her to own it. Matthew put on his seatbelt, and Cole was already in a car seat; I started the car and heard Matthew laugh in the backseat.

"What is it, Matthew?"

"Mommy," he giggled, "there's a vegetable in the floor."

When we arrived at the low-income housing apartment, I got Cole out and looked. There was a mushroom growing from the carpet on the floorboard. I laughed and told Matthew that the windows don't roll up all the way so I guess the carpet got wet and decided to grow a mushroom. We laughed as we walked through the new complex to the manager's office. I came in and she was a large woman, she didn't seem to like children or look too happy but from the tone of her voice, I could tell she was a smoker. She had shelves filled with collector dolls and looked daringly at Matthew as if to warn him not to touch a thing.

"So, you're here for the low-income unit?"

"Yes," I replied.

"So, where do you attend school or work?"

"I don't," I replied.

She took a look at me and my kids, raised a painted-on eyebrow and said, "Where's their dad?"

I felt embarrassed to tell her my story so I just said, "He died."

I think this gave her a reason to give me — to give us — a chance. This was going to help me get on my feet, sign up for school, and find a job. I wanted to show I was responsible and set a better example for my children. After I signed the lease and got the apartment keys, I walked out and felt proud. I lifted my head, held Matthew in one hand, and carried Cole in the car seat in the other all the way across our new complex to our old orange car that provided "soil" for a mushroom.

Moving day was not easy. I got a few of my neighbors to help me load the truck I rented, but when it came time to unload that was a problem, especially with two young children and an apartment unit upstairs. I decided to walk over to the manager's office and ask if she knew anyone who I could pay to help me. She looked frustrated as she put someone on hold. I noticed she was watching television. I suspected she was annoyed by the interruption since it appeared she was ordering another doll being held up by the model on TV. The large, almost life-sized doll had a detailed description with it. I noticed the office manager's nametag read, "Betty".

"Tim, Tim, Tim!" she screamed into the phone three times, but it turned out she wasn't screaming at the person on the phone.

A nice, friendly looking thin man ran up and seemed happy to see us.

"Yes, Betty?"

"Tim," she paused to cough, "Tim, can you take a break and help our new tenants unpack their truck, please?"

I was surprised she hadn't asked for money and smiled at her excited for the free help.

Tim followed me and the kids to the rented truck. As we talked, I noticed that he was just an average-looking guy with dark hair and a mustache. He dressed in jeans, old tennis shoes and a plain, white shirt, no jewelry — not even a watch. Tim asked all sorts of questions about me, my goals and visions for the future. It was nice to have a new friend, especially one who seemed to really care. He said he had worked for the apartment complex for nine years and did all the cleaning after tenants left and fixed anything that went wrong like on the garbage disposal. He said he also lived near us in an apartment, and if we ever got locked out or needed anything, he was the go-to guy. He smiled at me, and I asked if he was married or had any kids.

"No, I am a sort of loner guy. I just work and keep to myself."

He looked down at Matthew and rubbed the top of his head.

He continued, "I would love to have kids of my own but just haven't found the right person."

He smiled at me, which caused me to blush and look at the ground. I hoped he didn't think I was asking for him to get together with me. "He is a nice guy but not my type," I thought to myself as we walked across the apartment.

He asked me, "What about you? Are you married?"

I looked at him surprised and said, "No, I am raising my kids alone. Their dad died in a car accident."

Matthew interrupted and said, "I wish I had a dad to play with me."

Tim and I exchanged glances, and we both stopped talking. Tim helped me bring all the furniture into our new apartment, and I thanked him.

I also said, "I would buy you dinner, but I haven't unpacked my food, and I have no money. Plus, I am exhausted and need to take care of the baby. Thank you so much though, Tim, you are a lifesaver and I mean that."

Tim stood at the door and looked over at Matthew, "Okay

kid, what if you and I go to Mc D's and give your mom a little time to settle in. We'll bring her back something to eat?"

Matthew got up and started to jump around all excited to go to a place I could rarely afford to take him. I felt it was such a kind offer, and I was about to say no but remembered I had not unpacked the food, and Cole was crying to be nursed. I relented and agreed to let Matthew go. They left a few minutes later.

I woke up to find myself asleep on the couch with Cole also asleep in my arms. Tim was having trouble unlocking the door with his key. I got up and opened the door; Tim looked tired and held Matthew.

Tim said, "I know it's late but boy does your son have energy. He played and played before I knew it, it was dark. I hope you weren't worried. Oh, here's your food."

As he handed me a bag, I lay Cole down on a blanket and took Matthew from Tim. I noticed how dirty Matthew looked.

"Thank you so much again, Tim, I really appreciate it and don't know what I would have ever done without you."

I locked the door behind Tim and smiled down at Matthew. I carried him to his bedroom. His bed was the only one I'd had time to set up. A toddler bed with super-hero sheets. Matthew and Cole were to share a room, but it was a large room that was just down the hall from mine, and it had a window that faced the street and a large balcony the kids could play on.

"Tomorrow after breakfast, you, my child, are getting a good bath," I said as I kissed him and covered him with his super-hero sheet.

I sat by his bed and looked at his face. I wondered if his dad Michael was with us that night as I felt a cold breeze and knew life would only get better. Smiling, I walked out of Matthew's new room and closed the door behind me.

"Tomorrow I will set up the crib," I thought to myself.

Chapter Eighteen

The following morning, I got up before the kids to set up Cole's crib. Cole was the first to wake up and want to nurse. I felt so lucky to have such an easy baby in Cole. All I had to do was put a few toys on the floor, and Cole would be happy to play as he looked at us. He didn't need to be constantly held like Matthew. It was a good thing that Cole came second because I felt bad enough that Matthew had to share our time with Cole since he was used to having me all alone.

After making breakfast, I went to wake up Matthew. He had already slept over 12 hours and didn't want to get up. I convinced him we would play together after we ate and he took a bath; then he agreed to get going. He walked funny to the kitchen, but I knew yesterday was a long day. He said it hurt him to sit on the chair, but I started to lose my patience with Matthew so he relented, sat down, and ate his breakfast. After breakfast I told Matthew it would be a good idea to take a warm bubble bath and that would relax his tired little body. I helped Matthew get undressed. I noticed and felt concerned about some dark brown and red poop stains in his underwear.

"That's strange," I thought.

I decided our diet needed to improve, and we would have to add more vegetables to our meals. I gave Matthew a bath and washed his legs and noticed all the bruises.

"Gee Matthew, you sure played hard at Mc D's," I commented. "That was nice of Tim to take you."

Matthew didn't say anything, but I knew he was tired.

It was the summer before Matthew started the first grade. We went to the apartment pool and swam most days, took walks to parks, or just stayed home and watched TV. I got a job as a cocktail waitress in the evenings so I could stay home with my boys during the day. My godmother or Tina came to watch the kids until I found a neighbor to pay $20 for the night to watch them. Her name was Nora, she was nice and on social security so she could use the extra money. I think she would just come over, watch TV, eat, and ignore my kids, but it was better than leaving them alone, and she was the only one I could afford. Nora had been married several times and had many children whose fathers ended up raising them for different reasons; but Matthew and Cole seemed fine with her — and as long as they were fine, I felt fine, too.

I worked six nights a week and found it difficult once Matthew started school to get up in the mornings, get him ready, and pack up Cole to drive across town and back. So Tim offered to help. Matthew was upset because he wanted me, but I told him it was safer for Tim to take him because Mommy worked so much and was so tired that she couldn't even see straight. It made things easier to just get up to feed and dress Matthew and let Cole sleep until Tim would arrive to get Matthew. Tim never charged me for gas and always showed up early. Sometimes he even took Matthew to Mc D's for breakfast so I wouldn't even have to cook.

Cole got really sick one day and couldn't move from the couch to crawl so I called the free clinic and told them about it. They said to watch him and if he got worse to bring him to E.R., but they didn't have any appointments until the next week. I couldn't believe Cole could look any worse; he was blue and couldn't move. I looked at him and reminded him he would be all right. After a while Cole, who could barely speak, asked me to take him to the doctors. I decided it was time to go to the E.R. so I packed Cole's things and dialed Tim to ask him if he would pick up Matthew from school, and he agreed.

I took my time getting Cole to the E.R.. When I arrived a nurse looked at Cole and screamed out some numbers, and the next thing I knew someone dressed in blue grabbed Cole from my arms and left me standing there at the front desk. The nurse asked why I waited so long to bring my baby in, and I told her that I tried to call the free clinic but they couldn't see him until next week.

She made me have a seat and said, "Well, he doesn't look good. I hope he makes it."

"What do you mean?" I asked surprised.

She replied, "He is blue and lifeless. I have seen my share

of children pass away from asthma, but I have never seen one still alive that blue."

I sat and cried and wondered what took me so long to drive to the E.R.? Why didn't I just go right away? I thought about the last visit to the E.R. when the school told me that Matthew had lice. I brought him to the E.R. and waited for several hours just to have a doctor yell at me for bringing my kid in for something that I could have bought over the counter at a drug store. I didn't know (and I knew I had low-income insurance through the state), but I was afraid to go back to the E.R. after that incident. So, I sat and waited all night and for two days as Cole lay in a hospital bed with machines to breathe for him. I didn't want to go home — and thank God Matthew was safe with Tim.

Chapter Nineteen

Cole was on a nebulizer and had to have daily treatments, but he was improving. I learned so much about asthma — a disease that I knew nothing about and had never even heard about. To make matters worse, I had started school but had to take care of my children, and I felt so guilty that I dropped out. Despite these obstacles, I still had a vision of becoming a professional businesswoman — someone my children could be proud of.

Soon it was time for Matthew's first parent-teacher conference — and it didn't go too well. The teacher was disappointed in Matthew because he withdrew from the other kids, he wasn't able to sit still, and he refused to take a nap.

The teacher said, "I caught him taking a plastic penguin and putting it in his backpack. He is always late to school every day."

I was more surprised to hear that because Tim showed up early enough to get him there on time. I told the teacher that I would make extra effort to discipline Matthew and drive him to school myself each morning. When I got home, I took all

Matthew's super-hero action figures and put them in a box up in my closet. I told him he was in trouble for being late for school and not minding his teacher.

Matthew looked sad, and I continued, "From now on, Tim is not to drive you to school anymore. I don't care how tired I am, I am going to drive you myself."

Matthew got up from the floor, wiped his tears, and jumped into my arms.

He hugged me and said, "Oh thank you Mommy."

I was surprised and looked at Matthew who had stopped crying, smiled, and continued, "Now, Tim won't make me suck his penis anymore."

I was shocked and pushed Matthew off my lap and yelled at him, "Tim would never do that. That is nasty and disgusting. You are never to say that again! I don't know what I would do without all Tim's help so you mind him when you're with him and you mind your teacher, too!"

I walked out of the room upset, slamming the door behind me. I left Matthew to think about his behavior. I went into the other room and heard the door knock; it was Tim.

I opened the door still upset and said, "Look Tim, I don't know what's going on, but Matthew is always late for school and from now on, I am going to drive him. I really appreciate all you have done for us, but I don't need your help anymore."

Tim looked shocked and tried to talk, but I had no more patience and really didn't want to hear what he had to say so I smiled and shut the door.

A few days later, my godmother Sherry came to visit and mentioned a man hanging around the street below my apartment when she walked up; he was looking up into the window.

"I know it's this guy Tim. I used to let him help me all the time with Matthew, and he has this huge crush on me, but I decided to tell him to leave me alone. He's starting to give me the creeps, and I might have to get a restraining order against him."

Sherry said, "It's too bad, he's a nice-looking guy, and he must really like you to be hanging around your apartment all the time."

I just smiled and agreed. "Matthew's been on restriction for acting up in school. I get up four hours after I go to bed to take him to school. I am so tired. Between work, Cole's asthma, and Matthew misbehaving, my days go by so quick. I am just exhausted every day."

"Parenting is never easy, is it?" Sherry interrupted, smiling as she helped me fold the third load of dried laundry.

"Matthew is also having nightmares every night and wetting the bed. I get home from work around three in the morning and am so tired, my feet hurt, my back and arm hurt, and I just beg for sleep, but I can't because I hear Matthew tossing around and crying from these horrible nightmares. I scream from my bed for him to just be quiet, but I am just too tired to get out of bed and comfort him. My body hurts, and I can't see straight. It's hard enough I have to get up and take him to school early. He's always too tired to wake up. Mornings are another story of yelling to just get him up and dressed. The teacher said he won't take a nap and if he does, she can't get him to wake up."

Sherry got up, gave me a hug, and said, "You'll get through it. Having another baby might be difficult for Matthew to have to share your attention."

As Sherry walked out, Nora came in.

"Oh, it's that time already. I told you, Sherry, the days just go by so quick."

Nora said the neighbors all had been talking about my affair with Tim.

"I guess Tim said you let him do all these things for you and used him. Then you just dumped him."

"What?" I replied, "That's just plain crazy."

I began thinking about all the times Tim had come around and wanted to make me happy and why I never noticed how much he liked me.

"Anyway Matthew has been having nightmares and wanting to sleep in my room. I don't understand that kid, he was such a sweet boy and now he's different. Have you noticed anything?" I asked.

Nora probably didn't care. All she did was pay attention to the TV. She didn't even hear me ask her that question. I got ready, kissed my kids, and reminded them to obey the sitter and to do everything she said. Then I left and walked fast to my car too worried I would be late again for work.

When I came home that night and paid Nora, I went to

check on Matthew and Cole. Matthew was still awake.

"Mommy, please let me sleep in your bed," he begged.

I looked at Matthew and said, "Matthew, what is wrong with you?"

"Mommy, it's Tim. He wants to get me."

I stood up and checked the window.

"See Matthew, it's locked. No one can get in here to get you."

But I let Matthew come sleep in my bed, even though I was against bed sharing after a child turns three. I just felt they needed to learn to be secure on their own. He grabbed my neck all night, refused to let go, and continued to have nightmares. The next morning, I noticed the boys' door was open and Cole was still sleeping. I looked at Cole, and he had a bloody lip. I was surprised and figured he must have gotten up and fell on the crib rail. I went to make breakfast and noticed I forgot to lock the front door after Norma left.

"That's strange," I thought as I got Matthew ready for school.

I packed Cole's diaper bag. On the way to the car, I noticed Tim stared at us. I told Matthew that after I dropped him off at school, I was going to get a restraining order so he would have to stay away from us. Matthew squeezed my hand as we walked to the car. Later I contacted the police and started the process to get a restraining order. It didn't go very well. I did get the restraining order, but all the good that did me. The police had initially tried and failed to catch Tim in the act, which didn't help my case.

"But I have called over and over and you guys always show up after he's gone!" I complained.

"Sorry lady," the police officer said, "we have to catch him harassing you."

"He's always standing on the street, staring up at our windows. It creeps me out, and there's nothing you can do? Why did I even bother to get a restraining order?"

The police officer suggested I speak to the apartment manager, but I knew that would be no use. I couldn't start trouble around there; I needed the reduced rent and couldn't afford to move.

"Thank you officer," I said as he turned to walk down the steps to leave.

"Matthew, how about you, me and Cole take a walk to Mc D's and get dinner?"

Matthew was so happy to get his shoes on and leave.

"He's been so much better and improved each day," I thought. "I must be doing something right."

As we walked with Cole in one hand and Matthew in the other, I said, "Matthew when we get home, I am going to let you have your superhero-action figures back."

Matthew looked up at me smiled and said, "I love you Mommy."

We had a great time that night at Mc D's, the kids played for hours.

That night, after the kids got their baths, I helped them

brush their hair and teeth. I looked at Matthew's penis; it had bubble blisters all over it. It must be an infection from the circumcision, I thought.

"All right, kids, get dressed and grab a few toys; we need to go to the E.R. and have them check on Matthew's blisters," I said.

I drove to the E.R. as fast as I could since I was worried about it. The receptionist recognized us and looked at me like, now what? I checked in, and we waited. The doctor greeted us and introduced himself as Dr. Wax. He said he had been a pediatrician for 30 years. He was a kind person. He walked toward me, leaned forward, and extended his hand for a slight shake. Dr. Wax put on some glasses and asked Matthew if it was all right if he checked the blisters. Matthew looked at me as he pulled down his pants and the doctor did an inspection. The doctor looked down and froze still as he examined Matthew's penis. Dr. Wax stood up with a sad face, turned, and looked right in my eyes. He asked me point blank if I knew Matthew was being molested. I felt dizzy and blacked out.

Chapter Twenty

My eyes opened enough to get a glimpse of a white room as my head spun uncontrollably. I tried to lift my head off the pillow to look for my kids, but each attempt just made me even dizzier to the point of throwing up then passing out. Each time I woke up, I looked for Matthew or Cole and sometimes tried to call their names. I knew I was still at the hospital, and I knew I was now the patient, but I had no idea how long I had been in this condition or how long it would last. I felt scared and I wanted to wipe my chin from the vomit but realized my hands were tied down on each side of the hospital bed. I opened my eyes to look up as I saw a dark-haired woman walk in to check on me.

"Hello," I said.

Then my head spun back, and I turned to throw up.

"Well, hello to you. My name is Rocio. Can I ask if you know who you are?"

I smiled as she wiped my chin and used another warm cloth to clean the rest of my face.

"Rocio, I am worried about my kids, Matthew and Cole. Can you please tell me where they are? My name is Jen," I managed to reply.

"Jen, your kids are fine. Your mother picked them up yesterday."

"What!" I screamed.

I began to cry. I was worried sick, and I couldn't get control of my dizziness.

"Your mother was very concerned about you, Jen. She showed up right away and was happy to help you. She is such a delight," Rocio said with a big smile.

Rocio had no idea how crazy mother could be or how worried I was for my children. Rocio seemed to be a kind, patient woman and probably never had to think about child abuse.

"Rocio, I need to get better so I can get my kids. Do you know how long I am going to be dizzy for?"

"Jen, you had an 'adjustment disorder,'" she said and got closer to my face. Her smile changed to a serious expression as she whispered, "Nervous mental breakdown. You'll probably be here a while. Think of it as a break. Time to recover. They'll probably want you to talk to the psychologist, and I know Child Protective Services needs to meet with you."

I knew there was nothing I could do. I couldn't leave, I couldn't drive if I did leave, and I had no one to call who would understand the situation with my mother who could help me get my kids. I didn't trust anyone anymore, and the more I worried, the dizzier I got. I needed to focus on getting healthy so

I could get my kids. There was nothing more I wanted than to hug Matthew and tell him how very sorry I was for not believing him about Tim. How I missed them and couldn't wait to hug them and hold them; and to keep them close and protect them.

Rocio gently took the straps off my arms and lifted my bed up.

"Now, isn't that better?" Rocio asked with excitement.

At that moment, I began to really focus on Rocio, and I noticed how she was such a tiny person almost like a young school-aged girl but probably near my mother's age of 40.

"I'll do what I can to help you. Now let's get you to take this medication and start working on exercises to get you better."

I worked as hard as I could with the help of Rocio although it took several times to just take a single step without falling. It took a few days, but I was up walking and able to focus enough to meet with the psychologist. She was a large-framed, well-dressed woman. She walked into my hospital room and sat on the doctor's chair. She introduced herself as Tracy and asked basic questions about my background and living arrangements as she continually kept looking at her watch. Tracy seemed bored talking to me, like she had more important things to do. Truth was, I wanted to get my kids so I barely answered her questions.

She began to get more excited and interested as she sat up taller in her chair, rolling it next to me as I lay back in my bed. Tracy asked me more important questions like: Are you suicidal? After every answer I would ask if I could get my kids yet. Finally, she briefly left and returned with a phone.

"Call them" as she handed me the phone with a smile.

I couldn't dial fast enough.

"Hello Mother, how are the kids?"

Mother sounded agitated and replied, "You know after I had to drive down and get them because you can't handle stress, all you have to say is, 'How are they?' What about me? 'How are you, Mother?' would be a nice change.'"

"Mother, how are you?" I replied.

"Now, you ask?" she said irritably, paused, and finally replied, "Fine. How long do you plan to be there and expect me to babysit?"

"Mother, thank you so much for getting the boys. I really appreciate it. I hope they have been good."

"Well, I gave them good baths, they were so dirty, Jen. I added a few cups of Lysol so Matthew wouldn't pass any diseases to Cole."

"Mother, please don't give them any more baths. I'll be out soon, and I'll do that. Can I please talk to Matthew?"

"He's already sleeping. It's 9:00 p.m.," Mother snapped back.

"Okay, Mother. I'll try to get them tomorrow."

The phone went dead so I knew Mother had hung up first. I felt better since I knew the kids were all right but worried that Mother couldn't handle them for much longer.

Tracy took the phone and said, "Once you recover, I'll clear you to be dismissed. Good luck with your family."

I couldn't sleep that night. I laid helplessly in the hospital bed and prayed to recover so I could get out and get my kids.

I waited for hours the next morning for CPS to meet with me. The doctor came in several times to check on me, and Rocio came in even though it was her day off to check on me, say goodbye, and wish me luck.

She stood by my bed and whispered, "When you were out, you talked and talked. I was shocked at the things you said."

I looked at her, shocked, and wondered what I had said.

Rocio continued, "You should write a book. I would read it."

I couldn't help but smile at the thought. "Me, write a book? Who would read my book?"

I was more than ready to leave but was told I had to interview with CPS before they allowed me to be discharged. I asked Rocio if I could call my kids, and she got me the phone.

"I thought you would be here by now! Where the hell are you? You better get these kids before I kill them!" Mother screamed loud enough that even Rocio heard her.

I hung up and begged Rocio to help me; I needed to leave. She agreed and arranged for my discharge paperwork.

"Thank you, Rocio. You are an angel."

"Let me know when you write that book and stay strong, sweetie!" Rocio said in a louder-than-usual voice as I walked as fast as I could out the hospital doors and ran to my car. I still felt dizzy but knew I had to get my kids.

The kids were never so happy to see me when I showed up at Mother's house. I couldn't get them out fast enough, and I couldn't get them home fast enough. I did notice a cat and stopped to ask mother about it. Mother said it was pregnant, and she was waiting for it to have babies before she found them all a good home. I was concerned and even though I didn't want a cat, I asked mother if I could take the cat to help her since she helped me with the kids.

She agreed and said, "It's the least you could do really."

Mother said this as she helped me pack my car with the cat in a borrowed cat cage and a small bag of cat food. I drove home and kept looking at Matthew from the driver's mirror as he was sitting in the backseat next to Cole. He looked tired but happy to be going home. We pulled up to our apartment parking lot, and I was shocked to see Tim. He stood in a walkway and swept like nothing had happened. I pulled my car up to him and rolled down the driver's window.

I glared right at him to let him know I was pissed and yelled, "Hey, you child-molesting pervert. You stay the hell away from my kids or you'll be sorry!" I turned and looked Matthew in his eyes and said, "Do you want to yell anything to that bad guy?"

Matthew must have felt safe knowing I believed him and that I was going to protect him.

Matthew rolled down his window just a little and yelled, "You can't make me eat your banana or oranges anymore!"

My heart sank as we drove past Tim who stood there and looked shocked as we parked our car on the other side of the complex to avoid him. I felt awful for Matthew and knew I needed to press charges against Tim. I held Matthew's hand and the pregnant cat with the other with Cole following closely behind. We walked upstairs and went into our apartment. After I locked the door and pushed our old brown couch against it for extra protection, I got on my knees and hugged Mathew tight. I looked him in the eyes.

Matthew told me, "Mommy, now he's going to kill you. He said if I told you he would kill my mommy."

I knew Matthew had tried to be brave before, and I didn't listen. I felt guilty and unhappy with myself and told Matthew, "I am not afraid of Tim at all. I am very mad at him for hurting you, and I am mad at myself for not believing you. He lied to you; he can never hurt me, so don't you worry about Mommy. Tim will not be allowed near you ever again. Mommy is going to the police, and we're going to have them take Tim away and lock him up in jail."

Matthew smiled and hugged me even tighter. I was secretly scared. Matthew and Cole slept on my bedroom floor in a child's tent with the light on for weeks. I lost my job from missing so many days, which was fine because I didn't want to be away from my kids, not for a minute.

Chapter Twenty One

Betty, the manager, called me in to her office. I walked down the stairs as I carried Cole and held Matthew's hand tight. As we walked, I thought of how the office manager would tell me how sorry she was and that she would fire Tim right away. I opened the office door and sat down. I put both kids on my lap and waited for Betty to get off the phone.

She hung up and gave me a long stare from across the large oak desk, "I hear you have been harassing my employee," she said as if she were very upset with me.

I was shocked and responded, "He molested my son, and I plan to press charges."

She looked down, began taking notes of what I had said, and added, "Your rent just went up an additional $120 a month."

"But I lost my job over this and can hardly afford it as it is."

I was upset trying to hold back my tears.

"Well, you better get a job."

She took her pencil and swished it at us as if to let us know she had nothing else to say and we were to leave.

As I got up Matthew blurted out, "Mommy look! She has no eyebrows."

I looked at Betty as her large, painted eyebrows lifted in anger, and her face became beet red. I didn't know what to say to Matthew, he had already been through so much that I didn't want to discipline him so I just whispered to him not to blurt out people's flaws.

"What did you just say?" Betty screeched. "My flaw? Your rent just went up $150 a month so how do you like that? Now, if I hear you continue to harass my employee or spread rumors that aren't true, you will get an eviction notice!"

I knew there was no use in saying anything. I picked up Cole, held Matthew's hand, and decided it was time to go to the police station. I walked to my old, orange car and knew who had punctured the tires, all four. So, we walked and I tried to hide my tears as I held my kid's hands tight the six blocks to the police station. Neither Matthew nor Cole complained once about the long walk. I wanted to move; I couldn't afford to move. I had nowhere to go and no one to help me. I felt alone, scared, and couldn't wait to get some help from the police. I knew how much they had helped me in the past in the other town and knew that this town wouldn't be much different. They would do something to help us now. "That's why they're here, to serve and protect," I thought as we walked.

As I opened the door, two officers stood at the door as if they were expecting us. I went to the information desk and asked the clerk if I could file a complaint and press charges against a man at our apartment complex.

She sat and looked at me, rolled her eyes back, and yelled over to the two police officers, "This is that girl Betty warned us about."

The police officers walked over to us and asked to take Matthew to the backroom.

"I don't feel comfortable being without him," I anxiously said.

I was worried, this didn't seem right. The shorter police officer spoke up and said he was going to ask him questions while recording him, and I couldn't be there. He said, "It was standard practice."

So, I told Matthew to go with the police officer, and I would wait for him right where I was. As Matthew walked off and followed the police officer, the other police officer asked me to follow him into the other room. I questioned him, but he insisted he wanted to talk to me. I went and sat on a chair. I held Cole on my lap, and the police officer sat down on a chair across from me.

"So, why are you causing so many problems?"

I was surprised as he continued, "This is a small community, and we don't need welfare mothers starting rumors and harassing a well-respected tax-paying member of our community. Tim goes to our church and would never do such a thing!"

Standing up and feeling more shocked, I became very angry. I picked up Cole who was now sitting in front of me on the floor playing with a few toys I had brought.

I walked out shaking and yelling at the police officer, "You are supposed to protect the innocent! Instead you're accusing me of harassing a man who betrayed my trust and stole my child's innocence!"

I ran down the hall with Cole in-hand straight to the room where I knew Matthew was being questioned, but it was locked. I began pounding on it. The police officer opened the door with Matthew who followed behind. I could see Matthew had been crying. I grabbed Matthew's hand and slammed the police-station's door on our way out. We walked home.

Matthew looked up at me and said, "Mommy, are you mad at me or the police man? He said I was a bad boy. Am I? Am I bad boy, Mommy?"

I stopped, bent down, and hugged my son tight, "No Matthew. You are not bad; you are a sweet, wonderful child. I am so proud of you for being so brave. Tim is the bad guy, and we'll find a way to prove that."

We walked slowly up the stairs, opened the apartment door, and just when I thought I had enough, I saw feathers scattered all over the apartment family-room floor. The cat I took from Mother's house had had her babies, and I had forgotten to feed her. She had gotten my special parakeet Timmy. I could see Timmy had put up a fight, and I couldn't blame the cat for being hungry, but it gave me even more reason to scream, cry and sleep all the remainder of that day.

Later I called my real father Dave whom I hadn't spoken to in years. I tried to tell him about Matthew and my car. I explained I needed new tires so I could find another job and avoid a cross-town bus ride with two kids to take Matthew to school.

"Are you calling me after all these years to ask for money, Jen?"

"Yes, Dad. I know it's been a long time, but I have been busy working with two kids alone."

"Well, I am not just going to give you money," he said. He paused and continued, "You can earn it. But, you have to earn it with a massage, sex, something else I want, like drugs."

I hung up on my father. I was shaking and upset. I was desperate so I called my mother. She answered, and I tried to tell her about my day, but she said she was tired and didn't have time for my problems. Before she could hang up, I asked her for $25 so I could buy bread, eggs, and milk.

She paused and replied, "I think I have done enough for you. You never even ask about me. I am the one struggling with my health. I bet you didn't even know that I have cancer. I have months to live. I am going to die, Jen, but all you care about is yourself — and you're young, you can get a job!"

I listened to Mother as she went on and on about her health, but anxiety got the best of me and I blacked out. I later awoke to the sound of Matthew crying. He was climbing up the counter and trying to get food but he fell. I realized I had not even fed my kids that day so I got up to make them food, but there wasn't much so they had crackers and peanut butter with water.

I decided it was time to look for a place to get groceries and opened the phonebook. I called a program called WIC (Women, Infants and Children), and they immediately gave us vouchers for eggs, milk, peanut butter, cereal, fruits and vegetables. I also filled out a form for a chance to win a free turkey at Thanksgiving, which was just a month away.

"I've never even cooked a turkey," I told the lady who gave me the WIC vouchers. "I am going through tough times, but it'll get better."

I tried to convince her, but she just stared at me and smiled.

I was able to sell my old car for enough money with my welfare to pay the rent. This left me with no funds to pay the utilities so I made a flyer and went to a drug store to make copies. I went door-to-door passing out the flyers on doorsteps in the rich neighborhood just blocks away from our apartment with my children, trying to find someone who might need their house cleaned or a babysitter. One woman saw me at her door and opened it. I recognized her as the woman who gave me the WIC vouchers the other day. She told me her name was Mrs. Anderson. I told her I was trying to get work to pay my utility bill. She immediately let me in her home and told me she desperately needed her house cleaned, and she would even watch my kids while I cleaned. Although I was scared to trust anyone with my kids, I knew I would be in the same house. I needed money so our power wouldn't be turned off so I agreed to clean her house.

Mrs. Anderson's house was already very clean so it wasn't hard work at all. Before I was even done, she gave me a check to pay my utility bill and gave us a ride home. She sent us home with a bag of apples and some cookies for the kids. I think besides my foster mother Camille, she was the nicest person I had ever met. The next day, Mrs. Anderson called me and said we won the turkey. It was to be delivered that week with all the fixings for the best Thanksgiving ever. The kids and I were so excited we had something to look forward to!

As days went by, I wondered why no one had contacted me about the charges I asked to press against Tim. I called the police station and was told by the same receptionist that they found Tim had done nothing wrong based on the taped conversation with Matthew. I hung up and knew they had no plan to charge Tim. I had to do something. I couldn't let Tim get away with what he did to my son. I opened the phonebook and began calling random numbers until someone told me to call Victims of Crime, which I did.

The response I received from them was amazing. They sent someone to my apartment right away. His name was Pat rick, and he was an obviously gay man, tall, dark, handsome, and and unavailable — at least to me. As he sat on the used, army-green floral couch I had purchased from a garage sale with my tips when I was working, he took notes and asked several questions. He was soft-spoken but direct. He had me sign a form to allow them to pull Matthew's hospital records and the police report especially the recording they did with Matthew. I felt better since I knew he was going to help us.

We got to know Patrick so well over the next several months. We became best friends although I couldn't trust him or anyone with my children, but he respected my feelings. He was only there to walk me through the trials that would happen once he had collected enough evidence with the district attorney. Of course, this meant nothing to me. I didn't know what was about to happen but whatever it was, I wanted justice for Matthew. I wasn't going to let Tim get away with ruining our lives and my reputation as a mother.

Not only was my turkey with bags and bags of food delivered as promised, but Mrs. Anderson who also worked for JCPenney said they had also chosen us to be the family they sponsor for Christmas! A week after our big feast we began to see Mrs. Anderson several times a week. She brought us a Christmas tree, lights, decorations, and two really huge stockings. I couldn't stop crying. I was overwhelmed with happiness but also upset. Mrs. Anderson gave me a hug and asked why I cried so much. It was hard to talk, but I finally managed to let her know that I couldn't afford to fill such huge stockings.

She smiled and began to laugh as she wiped my tears and told me, "Jen, you just take care of those boys. I'll take care of those huge stockings. Santa is coming Christmas Eve, so you make sure you're here to let him in, okay?"

I was shocked and said, "You have already done so much."

Mrs. Anderson smiled and left.

I told Patrick the good news, and he was excited for us. He let me know that court was coming up, and I needed to be there.

"It's a trial, so you need to dress nice. I'll be with Matthew when he's with the judge, but you'll have to wait in the parent room."

"Why can't I be there, Patrick?"

"Because you don't need to know all the details of what happened to your son," he said in a matter-of-fact voice. Patrick paused and continued, "It's disturbing."

I called my sister Tasha. I hadn't spoken to her in so long. We talked for hours, and she listened to me. I had no idea that she had her own problems. She told me that her face had been disfigured from a pit-bull that attacked her at mother's house.

"Mother has been so tired with her cancer but she keeps grooming rescue dogs from the garage sink Dad set up for her, and one dog was growling so Mother got frustrated while I was there. She demanded I get the dog that got loose in their yard. When I went to grab the dog, it bit my forehead and used its claws to grab my head. I had 384 stitches in my face and head."

"Why didn't Mother tell me?"

I was upset and shocked as Tasha continued, "Mother says it was my fault — the dog was scared, and I should have talked softly to the dog and not just grabbed at it. It happened so fast. I blacked out and awoke after surgery. Mother is angry at me after all she's done for me. I can't even get a modeling job. My career is over."

I felt awful for poor Tasha since her life was based on her gorgeous looks.

"Mother won't have anything to do with me. She said I was nothing but trouble, and Mother hasn't paid my rent or bills, and I even got an eviction notice. I don't know what to do. I thought about selling my car but then what? I can't get a job looking like this anywhere. People just stare and laugh. I look like a walking creep show."

"Tasha, come live with us," I interrupted. "I'll share my room with you, and I could really use some help with these kids."

Tasha laughed and gave me her address.

"Come by tomorrow, I have something for you and I would like to see the kids. I love you, little sister."

Patrick came for a visit the next morning. He brought breakfast for the kids and a calendar for me to keep track of important days. I told him about my sister and how worried I was for her. He was sorry and agreed to give us a ride to her apartment so we could see her. It was a long drive so we talked about the up-and-coming trial. I remember Patrick repeated himself a lot since I had a hard time absorbing anything he had to say. I felt like I was walking in fog. A woman whose insides felt like an empty bottle.

When we arrived at the proper address, I was shocked. The apartment complex was beautiful. I thought, "Tasha must be really rich to live here."

I was further shocked when Tasha opened her apartment door. I couldn't recognize her with all the bandages that covered her swollen head. Her eyes were purple, puffy and sealed shut like Mother's eyes used to be when Father beat her.

"Tasha, I am so sorry," I said.

I wanted to hug her but couldn't because she was in so much pain. I was glad we brought her some food because Tasha looked so thin as if she hadn't eaten for God knows how long. Matthew and Cole hid behind me, too scared to approach Tasha, so Patrick offered to walk them to the apartment playground, and I agreed that it would be best. The kids were more than excited to go play since I rarely let them leave our apartment.

Tasha and I talked for an hour about Mother and all we had been through. Tasha kept apologizing to me for everything.

"We were kids, Tasha, we didn't know better."

The conversation continued until Patrick and the kids returned. I looked concerned at Matthew, but his face told me he had a good time. I was glad. Before we were about to walk out, Tasha handed me a pink slip signed in my name to her car.

"But Tasha, I don't want to take your car. You'll need to sell it to pay your bills."

Tasha managed a smile and replied, "I thought about it, and I'll be fine. I made other plans. You use it and take care of my nephews."

I knew Tasha was sore, but I wanted to leap out of my skin and hug her tight. I could tell she was tired and decided to blow her a kiss. I also made Matthew and Cole blow her a kiss, but I couldn't get them to talk to her at all. I know Tasha understood though.

That night Patrick and I celebrated and took the kids to a movie for the first time. We saw a new turtle action movie. Patrick had another surprise after the movie. He gave the kids the turtle action figures as an early Christmas gift. When we got home, Patrick told me that I had changed his life. He said if he wasn't gay, he would marry me and that he really cared about me and the kids.

I smiled, hugged Patrick, and told him, "If you weren't gay, I would marry you too. You are one amazing person!"

We looked at each other, laughed, and jumped as the phone rang. I got up to answer it; it was my father Dave.

"Jen, I wanted to let you know I have been thinking of you. I met this beautiful young girl your age, and she's been taking real good care of me. She looks just like you, Jen, exactly! Would you like to talk to her?"

I hung up and ignored the several calls that followed. I knew they were my drunken father. Patrick unplugged the phone on his way out and kissed me on the top of my head. He told me to get some sleep. I thanked him again and watched him walk down the stairs. I thought it really was too bad he was not interested in women.

Christmas Eve was here and as expected, a knock at the door.

"Who is it?" I asked through the door.

"Ho, ho, ho," we heard and opened the door with excitement as Santa walked into the apartment with JCPenney employees and Mrs. Anderson, who followed with bags of gifts. I was so excited, especially watching the kids with Santa. Mrs. Anderson and the employees sat on the avocado-colored couch all excited, too. We watched Matthew and Cole open the amazing donated gifts. I was surprised because they even had a stack of gifts for me. I opened an oak jewelry box and gift cards to the movies, Mc D's, arcade, and a certificate to the JCPenney's Portrait Studio for a free family photo. The kids got clothes, books, puzzles, treats, and comforters for their bunk beds. I had never had such an amazing Christmas. I would cherish that day for the rest of my life and use those huge stockings year after year. I also said a special prayer to God for sending us Santa that year.

Christmas day I asked Patrick if he would watch the kids so they could stay and play with their new toys, and I could visit Tasha for a few hours. Although I never trusted anyone with my children, Patrick seemed different. He never asked to spend alone time with them, and he genuinely cared about us in a way that was sincere. Patrick didn't have family. He, too, was alone this Christmas. His family had disowned him when he came out as a teenager and announced he was gay. They told him it was a choice, and he could choose to not be gay. Patrick stood by his belief that he couldn't change, and his parents kicked him out. I couldn't believe anyone could be so cruel. Patrick was the sweetest, kindest man I had ever known, and he was also very good looking.

I took the long drive in my new car Tasha gave me, pulled up at the fancy apartment complex, went to Tasha's door and knocked and knocked. I stood there, shocked that she wouldn't answer the door and even more shocked that the door was unlocked. I figured Tasha was tired from recovering from her surgery, and so I opened the door immediately and saw Tasha's lifeless body on the floor. Tasha had decided to take her own life by overdosing on prescription drugs. I ran over to her lifeless body to hold her — she was limp, weightless, and her scarred face had turned from purple to gray. I held her in my arms, cried and kissed her all over.

"Oh, Tasha. Oh, Tasha. Please don't leave me, Tasha."

After Tasha's death I fell into a deep, deep depression. I didn't have many emotions during my childhood, and now I had so many emotions my life was like an emotional fog. I found it difficult to even function.

Mother had Tasha cremated and was upset that Tasha had already given me her car. Mother sold all of Tasha's belongings except for her clothes. Mother said I could have them if I paid Mother back for what Tasha owed when I got a job, but Tasha owed her a lot more and should have given Mother the car, too. I was allowed to keep a small jar of Tasha's ashes, which I wore around my neck on a black choker during the trial with Tim. I talked to Tasha every day, and I told her everything. Sometimes even today when a butterfly comes close to my head or a soft wind blows gently on my face, I swear I can smell her.

Chapter Twenty Two

The trial was not what I had expected. It was like a real court case on TV. I was nervous, and Patrick told me not to worry. He was allowed to stay by Matthew's side while Matthew testified. I waited in the room off to the side of the court with Cole. I was surprised that Mother had agreed to go with me in case I needed help with Cole. We sat in that room until the judge ordered a break for lunch, and Patrick told me that the attorney for Tim asked Matthew the same questions over and over. He even tricked Matthew and had him hold a pen and didn't take it back so Matthew would be distracted. Matthew played with the pen and didn't listen to the attorney.

"Couldn't you take the pen away?" I asked Patrick.

"No, I can't be involved. I am only there for Matthew's moral support."

Court continued the same for four days. As mother and I waited patiently in the waiting area for any word on the trial, Patrick asked if we could talk after court that night. "There's more that I think you need to know, Jen. Matthew is really going to need some serious help after this trial is over." Patrick looked concerned but went back into the courtroom.

I was stunned that Mother came to all the trials. She and Cole formed a close bond that surprised me. After Tasha died, Mother had no one to talk to. She began going to Bible study in the evenings. She taught what she learned to Cole while we waited in boredom for hours. Cole seemed interested although I think he was too young to understand, but the two (Grandmother and grandson) got along great. I was a little jealous of the attention Mother gave Cole because she ignored me all those hours as we sat alone in the waiting area. I thanked Mother for continually going to the hearing, and she reminded me that she had to do it for her grandsons. She wanted to get to know them because she wasn't going to be around much longer.

"The doctors keeps finding more and more cancer," she said.

That week was a long, boring one, and Matthew missed school to be in court. I had Matthew work on his second-grade class assignments while Patrick and I went in the other room to talk. Patrick grabbed my hand and got all teary-eyed. It took him a while to take control of his emotions so I could understand him.

"Jen, he molested Matthew over and over for months! It all started the first night when you let Tim take Matthew to Mc D's! It continued each time Tim had Matthew alone. When you wouldn't let him watch Matthew anymore, he made a copy of the office manager's keys and watched you. Tim used the key to break into your apartment when he knew you would be sleeping and too tired from working so much to get up." Patrick paused, wiping more tears and said, "They found videotapes in Tim's apartment of the 'games' he made Matthew play, and he tortured Matthew!"

"What!" I screamed back in Patrick's face.

"He used his key, snuck in when you were asleep, and woke up Matthew. He held his eyes open and used a flashlight to shine it in his face. If Matthew tried to blink, Tim poked Matthew's eyes. Matthew screamed, but it's worse, Jen, because we could hear you scream 'shut up' to Matthew! The entire jury is disturbed. They watched Tim tape Matthew being molested while Cole watched."

"Oh God. My baby."

I ran out to the kitchen table where Matthew was doing his homework, and I held him while I cried.

"Mommy, what's wrong now, Mommy?"

"Mommy just loves you so much, baby. Mommy is so sorry she didn't protect you in our own home. Mommy is so sorry she let that bad man come near you."

Matthew just continued his homework and didn't say a word.

Patrick said, "There's more. The list of abuse goes on and on. Tim pleaded 'No contest.'"

"Will he go to jail forever?"

Patrick looked at me and said, "This is one of the worst cases I have seen but because Matthew is alive, Tim will probably get less than 10 years."

Patrick was still crying as he said goodbye to us and

reminded us we had the next day off and to rest over the weekend; he would see us first thing Monday morning for sentencing.

I drove Matthew to school on time with his homework and walked him to the class to explain to his teacher what he had been going through. Although she seemed to look at me strange, I didn't care. The entire town heard rumors, and I couldn't even go to a store without someone commenting about the problems I caused. I couldn't tell anyone about the court case or the evidence the detectives had found because it would ruin my case, and then Tim would be free and charges would be dismissed. I only had Patrick and the remains of my sister Tasha to talk to. Patrick had other cases but this one took priority he would say.

I put my hand on the jar that held Tasha's ashes and began to ask her for help. I couldn't stop the evil feeling that I wanted to kill Tim. Then one afternoon temptation presented itself. As I stopped at a red light, I was aghast to see Tim walk right in front of my car and across the crosswalk as if nothing was wrong. He was in a great mood and looked up to talk to heaven — he didn't even notice me.

"How dare you look up and talk to God," I thought.

Tim slowly walked right in from of my car, the car Tasha gave me, and without even thinking and with my heart racing, I pushed my foot on the gas pedal as hard as I could and hit Tim.

I was charged with attempted murder with an armed weapon and imprisoned in a small jail cell with a cold concrete floor, bunk beds with thin mattresses, and a metal sink and toilet combination with no windows. After what seemed like weeks but was probably only days (I couldn't tell because the one light never went off in the cell), I was told by the guard who brought my food that Tim was alive with only a broken arm but bruised pretty bad. I was allowed out with my hands and ankles cuffed to make one call from a glass booth.

I sat in the booth and dialed Patrick. Patrick let me know that he had my kids and that they missed me, but they were doing just fine. Court had been delayed, and he would find out when I would meet with the judge about my charges. He assured me he would be there. I told him I wanted out of the jail cell.

"It's driving me crazy, the light is always on and I wake up and hear screams from other cells. I keep thinking it's Matthew and wake up panicked. I keep getting gang-member roommates who try to touch me when I sleep and stare at me when I pee."

"Jen, I'll see if I can talk to one of the attorneys I know quite well. We'll see what we can do."

After days had passed, a guard opened my door and pointed to an elevator. As I approached it, I was astounded to see my mother. She was upset and said she couldn't believe all the trouble I had caused. She said I was all over the news and papers, and the whole town talked about me. I was upset and scared but anxious to see my kids.

Mother dropped me off at the apartments and added, "I know you had no one else to call."

I walked up the steps and noticed an eviction notice posted on the door. I was too exhausted and only wanted to take a shower and see my kids. I was upset for hitting Tim, but I knew it was over and nothing could change what I did. I could only pray that I didn't ever have to sit in a cold cell away from my kids ever again. I couldn't believe I was happy that Tim didn't actually get too hurt because I knew he would finally be sent to jail. I knew how a week felt, and 10 years for Tim actually sounded good. I probably would have been sentenced to more time than him if I had actually killed him anyway.

I was allowed to sit in the court as Tim glared at me while we listened to the judge speak, "You were charged with aggravated forcible sodomy, indecent assault, battery of a minor, and breaking and entering. You, Tim, are a master manipulator. You have convinced the community that you were the victim and turned an entire community against a woman who was trying to get justice for her young son, Matthew. You not only made this family's life a living hell, but I found your behavior emotionally disturbing and for that, I sentence you to the maximum I am allowed by law: 10 years with the possibility of parole in six years with four years of probation. Tim, you violated a position of trust, and I hope and pray that God will be able to forgive you. If it were in my power, I would've locked you up for good!"

I looked over at Patrick and mouthed, "Thank you."

I knew because Tim hadn't actually killed my son that the

judge did what he could. I also wondered if God could forgive Tim. I didn't think I would ever be able to.

My court date arrived, and I was scared of what the judge was going to say to me. I was also scared I would have to leave my kids and sit in a cold cell. I wore one of Tasha's nicer outfits and walked into the courtroom. It took me by surprise that there was no jury, and it was the same judge who sentenced Tim. He sat up high behind a large cherry-wood desk and asked how I was doing. This took me by surprise, and I just fell apart. I couldn't answer; I couldn't get a word out to speak. The police officer to the side of me walked over and handled me a box of tissues.

The judge continued, "Jen, this is between us. I wanted to let you know that what happened to your son was tragic. I also wanted to let you know that when I was his age, my mother trusted a babysitter to care for me, and her husband molested me. The reason I tell you this is because I wanted you to know that you need to be strong for your son and support him when he needs it. Get Matthew involved in school activities and sports. Keep him in counseling and tell him every day that you love him. Now, about these charges, I am going to drop them, but you will not be allowed to purchase a gun, and you will be have two years of probation. I heard about your landlord, and I spoke to her in person. Betty has canceled the eviction. I informed her that if she continues to harass you, she will receive a lawsuit. I know attorneys."

I think the judge was trying to make me smile. As glad as I was for this news, I didn't think I had a smile left to offer.

"The police officer who taped Matthew no longer has a job and that goes for the police officer who threatened you as well. I spoke to the receptionist, and she told me everything after Tim was convicted."

I was speechless and managed to say, "Thank you, your honor."

He smiled and said, "Now, go take care of those boys; they need their mother."

He winked at me, and I went home to care for my damaged children.

Matthew and I both went through therapy for years after Tim's conviction in a program that Victims of Crime paid for. We still had dinner with Patrick several times a week sometimes being interrupted by Father's crank calls. I learned to laugh again, although not too often, and I got Matthew into modeling, where he was in several commercials. I wanted to get Cole into modeling, but he took after me and didn't have that "look". I sat back and watched Matthew smile for photographers and thought of how much he looked like Tasha. Even now I still miss her every day and hold her jar of ashes close — and sometimes I can even smell her or I think I hear her voice call my name, "Sister."

I had a hard time functioning for years, but Patrick helped and reminded me of the small things like writing a list to remind me of things like to make my bed, feed the kids — simple things that I would just forget. I couldn't believe how the years passed and Matthew was 12 and going to junior high. I had stopped talking to my mother, tired of hearing her stories of dying. We were still living in the apartment on welfare when Patrick came for dinner one night and wanted to talk to me.

"Jen, Tim has his first parole hearing and if he gets out, he'll be moving right back into these apartments, and there's nothing we could do to prevent that. He might be angry and come looking for Matthew or you. He may want to kill you, Jen, or even Matthew. I have an idea. I want you to marry me. Jen, will you marry me? I could get a job transfer, and you can change your last name. I could adopt your kids and change their last names so they could be safe. I could finally have the family I have always dreamed about, and your kids can finally have the dad they always wanted — and you will be protected."

Matthew must have heard because he interrupted and said, "Mom, if you don't marry Patrick, I am moving out of town with him because I never had a dad and Patrick is just like a real dad to me!"

It didn't take long for me to say, "Yes." Although it was awkward, I knew it was the right thing to do for my kid's safety and our future.

Chapter Twenty Three

Patrick and I had a small wedding and moved into a new three bedroom, two-bathroom single-story home in a small town hours from our apartment. I could watch the kids walk from our new home all the way to the school each morning. Patrick was able to adopt the kids without anyone contesting it, and we even changed their last names. The kids began to call Patrick Dad, and I felt like I was finally living life the way I should be with exception to the fact that Patrick had no desire to even kiss me, not even on our wedding day.

Every year on our anniversary, Patrick would find a reason to not be with me. I knew he felt bad, and I began to feel lonely over the years. I found a job at a furniture store and began working long hours. I volunteered at the kid's school on my day off. The other kids' mothers would make comments about how good looking my husband was and go on and on about his charming good looks and how lucky I was. I became more and more involved in the kids schools while making new friends, but never getting too close to anyone.

One day, I sat on our front lawn, pulled weeds, and planted flowers. A group of young boys Matthew's age walked side-by-side up our street. There were about 12 of them, and they looked like they were up to no good. I was happy to see them walk past me, but they stopped and asked for Matthew. I was scared and went into Matthew's room. Matthew lay on his bed and listened to music. He took his earpiece off to hear me tell him about the kids. Matthew went out front and walked down the street with the kids out of sight. I watched, worried and concerned and began to walk toward the boys when I saw Matthew skip up the street like he was happy. He skipped right back into his room and continued to listen to his music.

When the boys walked by and then out of sight I went into Matthew's room. I sat on his bed and asked him to tell me what that was all about.

Matthew sat up and like nothing was wrong told me about his day.

"There was a big play about abuse and rape at our school theater today," he explained. "They asked if there were any comments or if anyone wanted to share anything so I raised my hand and asked if I could go up on stage and share my story."

I looked shocked and felt my face become pale and said, "The whole school was there? What exactly do ... what did you say?" I nervously asked.

Matthew gave me a look like what's the big deal and continued, "I went up on stage in front of the entire school and told them about Tim and what he did to me."

My heart must have skipped a beat, and I was surprised after all the years how we taught Matthew not to talk about, "it," and we moved, changed our names to protect us and now, "The entire school knows?"

"Yep."

Matthew seemed real proud and had a big smile, and I said, "What did those kids want?"

"They wanted to know if I was gay."

Matthew began to turn around like it was no big deal.

I poked him and said, "So, what did you say?"

"I said, 'No.' Gee Mom, I am sure. So you think I am gay?"

I gave Matthew a kiss and said, "No way Matthew. You know when you were only three and I was pregnant with Cole, I would take long walks with you to the beach and you would see a lady wear a swimsuit and you would want to rub her legs saying, 'walk walks!' No Matthew, I know you are not gay!"

I smiled and went to the family room and waited anxiously for Patrick to come home to let him know what "his son" did today at school.

Patrick was shocked and a little concerned.

"What if they tease him at school? What is this going to do to his future?" he asked.

Patrick and I couldn't sleep that night worried for Matthew's up and coming days at school. I was pleasantly shocked at how well the school handled the news. I was called by the school office that next morning to come in to verify the horrific story, and I had to explain that if word got out of our small community the danger it could put our family in since Tim was now free from jail and had no idea what happened to us.

The weeks that followed were amazing and unexpected. Matthew began being included in all school activities and being invited to birthday parties. He was asked to try out for the school football team and got to be captain, and he won awards for track. His grades improved, and his confidence wasn't a concern because I could see he felt amazing, which was great. However, I was afraid that people who didn't know his past would not understand him in the future if his "confidence" continued.

Cole was proud of his older brother and also got involved in sports, and Cole even got a girlfriend before Matthew. I think Matthew had a secure attitude but deep down was actually shy.

I worked a lot and sold furniture for long hours while Patrick got home on time. He made sure the kids got home safely from school, helped them with their homework, took them to practices, and made dinner. By the time I came home, Patrick would be exhausted and already in bed. My dinner would be waiting for me, and I would have an hour to talk with Matthew and Cole before going to bed.

I was slowly trying to recover from depression and the overwhelming guilt from the past, but I was now suffering a different type of emotion — I was lonely. I couldn't watch TV without crying when I saw a couple kiss. I would try to get Patrick to just hold me, but I knew as much as he loved me that actually kissing me, which he did a few times, disgusted him as much as he tried to act like it was okay. I would often see him rush to the bathroom to brush his teeth. I was happy beyond belief for my family, but I needed more. I had a desire to be loved. I asked Patrick for a divorce.

At first Patrick was upset and begged me to stay with him. But I insisted it had to happen. I felt healed and desperate to find real love.

"We celebrated four anniversaries and seven years before marriage as friends. Sleeping in the same bed right next to a man who won't touch me is the most lonely feeling, Patrick!" I argued.

I looked him in the eyes and hoped he would understand.

I continued, "If you really love me, you'll let me go. I am ready!"

Patrick was always emotional but this day he was even more so, and he began to cry. Then he paused and asked me to wait until Matthew graduated and if I agreed, I could quit working at the furniture store where I was so unhappy working such long hours. I could spend full days to study the principles of real estate. I had dreamed of getting my real estate license for years. I was excited and agreed with prospects of a new future.

One morning after taking the kids to school, I decided to take a long drive alone to see Ann, the woman who had let me stay with her when I got pregnant with Matthew. I wasn't surprised that she couldn't remember me at all, but I could see the drugs had taken a toll on her face. She looked way older than her now-40-year-old age. I told her that even though she didn't remember me, I wanted to give her some money for taking me in and putting a roof over my head. I handed her a check for $1,000.

She thought it was some sort of scam, and I couldn't convince her otherwise. I gave her a hug and left. As I did so I took a look into her eyes. She looked tired, sucked in, and had scars from acne all over her once-beautiful face. It made me sad for her but glad that at least I didn't ever get into drugs.

I then drove to the high-end apartment Tasha had killed herself in. I sat on steps to her old apartment, and the door to her apartment opened. A woman walked out and saw me crying. I explained that my sister had once lived in her apartment and had since passed away. She let me in. I laid on the spot I once saw Tasha's lifeless body. I laid right there and remembered, crying and hugging her on the carpet. I looked up and could see the lady who looked at me strangely. I thanked her and decided it was time to go.

I then drove to the apartments where I raised Matthew and Cole for all those years. I was surprised to see a new office manager, who was much younger and friendlier. I asked her about Tim.

"He's still in apartment number one, living with his mother. She's not doing too well. He keeps to himself, and I have never seen anyone over there so I am sure they'll be surprised to have a visitor," she explained with a cheerful smile.

I thanked her and walked toward Tim's apartment and

shook with my heart racing. I remembered all the therapists over the years who had all agreed one on thing, forgiveness. I knocked at the door of the apartment with the number one on it. My hand trembled, and I was surprised to see Tim when he opened the door. He had aged poorly over the years. He looked exhausted and also resembled Ann with the sucked-in face and acne scars. He looked shocked to see me, even though I wasn't sure he even recognized me.

"I wanted to let you know I came over to forgive you for ruining my life, from stealing my son's innocence, and putting us through hell."

He seemed shocked and just stared at me.

I paused, looked at him, and continued, "But I can't. I could never forgive you for what you did to my child and to my family! You are a sick, mentally disturbed, poor excuse of a person, and I know you will rot in hell."

I turned to walk away and looked back, but Tim didn't say anything. He just stood there and then shut his door. I knew he probably molested many more innocent children. Even after all those years, I just couldn't forgive him. I would just have to accept that I hated that person and hope God would forgive me. I cried and walked back to my car, but knew I had one last stop.

Mother wasn't happy to see me at all, but I got to see my brother Jeremy, who was all grown up and was also there visiting. couldn't believe he was now an adult and living on his own. Jeremy had had quite a different experience with Mother, and we had never really spoken much. I asked Mother to step into the other room so we could talk.

"What's this about this time, Jen? Can't you see I have family visiting?"

Mother snapped as we stood in my old bedroom, which was now a sewing room.

"Mother look, you have changed and found religion, I am so happy for you. I have also changed so I am asking you to please forgive me for everything and anything I have ever done to make your life so unhappy and make you hate me."

Mother looked me in the eyes and said, "Jen, I could never forgive you for all you have put me through. You were supposed to be a boy, Jen."

I looked at my mother in her eyes and turned to leave.

"Jen, wait."

I stopped and hoped she would forgive me so we could start new; so I could have a normal mother-and-daughter relationship. I turned to look at her.

She said, "Maybe you could start paying me some of that money you owe me from that sports car you drove and all those fancy clothes of Tasha's you wore around."

I found it difficult but managed to smile, turned back to leave, and wondered if God had anything to do with Mother not forgiving me since I couldn't forgive Tim. I took the long drive home and decided I wasn't going to let things bother me anymore. I can't control other people. I can only control myself and be the best person I can. I decided to forgive myself.

Chapter Twenty Four

"The divorce happened after Matthew graduated with honors and I had passed my real estate exam on the first try. I even sold several homes. Patrick let me keep the money I had made for a deposit on a new home, and I agreed to let him keep our house and all its equity.

After I was all moved and settled in my new home, I met Jason at a friend's wedding reception. We had assigned seating at the same singles table. We just started talking and then danced all night. Someone thought we were already a married couple. We were inseparable from that day forward. Cole really liked Jason immediately, but it took Matthew a lot longer – he didn't want anything to do with Jason at first but things always have a way of working out."

I looked up at the kind nurse who had been there caring for me, listening to my life story, and rubbing my neck, face and temples as I talked and talked and talked. She was more than pretty – she was like an angel. She looked just like Tasha only an older and even more gorgeous version. She had perfect blonde curls and green eyes with long lashes, perfect fair skin with no blemishes, freckles or wrinkles. She just stood behind me with her white gown, looking down, smiling with her perfectly straight white teeth.

Then I felt it again, that same slow-moving, sucking-pull feeling that took me up and made me feel like a weightless feather and oh so good and free. It was the best feeling I had ever experienced. It was amazing — no stress, no problems, good health, happiness, and a sense of freedom like everything was absolutely perfect! Then I felt the crashing, pulling down like I was falling free high from the sky, and then down fast and hard out of control until my body felt a hard thump. I felt like I had hit the hard pavement with the entire back of my body. This continued to happen, this wonderful upward-pull feeling followed by the hard crash landing.

As I was going up, I saw the golden crystals swirl around me then crash down. I wanted the pulling-down feeling to stop and let go so I could go up and follow the golden crystals — the higher I got, the better I felt. I then realized that the kind nurse, the woman I had told my entire life story to all this time, had been reaching up and pulling me back down. Although I never saw her hands, she was why it felt as if I were crashing down so hard.

I wanted her to stop, but she kept whispering to me on my way down, "It's not your time to go. You have a story to share and a new life to celebrate."

This went on until my body became too tired to fight her,

and I relented. Then I looked over and noticed Jason, who sat across the room. He had a terrible look of sadness. He had crutches under each arm and a cast on one leg, and he was looking up as if he were praying.

"Jason, I am here," I repeated over and over until the doctor finally heard me and began examining my eyes.

He said, "We thought we lost you several times, Jen, welcome back."

Jason jumped up as fast as he could with his crutches and struggled as though he couldn't get to me fast enough. I looked up to thank my nurse, but there was just a headboard against a wall.

"Where's the wonderful nurse who was standing behind me helping me?"

"Well, aren't you happy to see your husband?" Jason asked, laughed with a huge smile, and wanted to immediately kiss me.

The doctor interrupted and said, "Give her time, she probably hallucinated. It's common when we lose people for them to imagine they experienced something or even talked to someone who never existed."

I was excited to go to our new home to recover from a fractured back. I learned that the man who hit us was a drunk driver; he was here on a work permit picking tomatoes with no insurance and no license. He ran a stop sign. After totaling a borrowed car, they found him walking away from the accident. He received four months in jail. Trixie, our dog, survived long enough to spend some time with me, but the pain became too much even with medication. She would just cry, and we were sad to let her go.

I thought about that nurse often and would never forget how much she looked like Tasha. I even wondered if she was my angel. When she told me I had a story to share and a new life to celebrate, I had thought she meant the new life with Jason. We had no idea at that time and later discovered that she was referring to the literal new life inside of me, as we were expecting. The day our new baby daughter was born we named her Tasha.

A Special Note from Author Jori Nunes

GAIL SHOOP-LAMY

Writing the story *Chocolate Flowers* was difficult for me to do emotionally; but it's a story I always knew I needed to write. Over the years I have discovered (as I am certain many other victims of crime would agree) that the topic of childhood sexual abuse is not a subject that most people feel comfortable discussing. I could never find a response to those who asked, "Why didn't you tell?" I can remember trying as a child to tell other adults. I even had adult authority figures make excuses for the predators by suggesting there was a "misunderstanding," followed by questions about what I did to cause the abuse or worse saying, she/he wouldn't do that. It sometimes even seems like society often treats the victim like he or she was somehow at fault and either invited or caused the abuse or molestation.

As a result, many victims of abuse hold their stories deep inside without receiving psychological treatment or some kind of intervention. With all these feelings and no help, sometimes victims turn to drugs or alcohol to self-medicate their pain. Others may lead productive lives (on the surface) while tucking away unpleasant memories and pain that later leads to severe depression, anxiety, anger, emotional breakdowns, headaches, suicidal thoughts or worse, suicide.

While interviewing pedophiles, I learned that boys are just as likely as girls to become victims of sexual abuse normally from an adult who first gains the family's trust and takes a special interest in an individual child. Predators control their victims through special gifts, vacations, outings and more. Then to prevent being "told on" they will threaten to take back gifts, harm loved ones, or convince the child that what the predator did was a natural act. They sometimes also tell children no one will believe them.

Society needs to teach children to respect parents, elders and authority figures, but also explain that in some cases that involve touch to a private area, "bumps" into their persons too many times, or inappropriate and ongoing "tickles" aren't always all right. We need to teach children to say "no" and practice saying "no" so it's not uncomfortable.

I am not a doctor or professional in the field of sexual abuse; but I am a parent of a sexually abused child and a victim of sexual childhood abuse. In these experiences, I am able to share this story and use my knowledge and share what's in my heart in hope that I am able to raise awareness on this important and critical subject. My greatest wish is that emotional, physical and sexual abuse never again be perpetrated on another innocent child.

A special thank you to Michelle Gamble, CEO of 3L Publishing, for her continued support, concern and assistance as she took this journey with me.

Jori Nunes
Chocolate Flowers